BONE'S

ENIGMA

by

KEN FARMER

Cover design by K.R. Farmer

AUTHOR

Ken Farmer didn't write his first full novel until he was sixty-nine years of age. He often wonders what the hell took him so long. At age seventy-seven...he's currently working on novel number twenty-seven.

Ken spent thirty years raising cattle and quarter horses in Texas and forty-five years as a professional actor (after a stint in the Marine Corps). Those years gave him a background for storytelling...or as he has been known to say, "I've always been a bit of a bull---t artist, so writing novels kind of came naturally once it occurred to me I could put my stories down on paper."

Ken's writing style has been likened to a combination of Louis L'Amour and Terry C. Johnston with an occasional Hitchcockian twist...now that's a combination.

In addition to his love for writing fiction, he likes to teach acting, voice-over and writing workshops. His favorite expression is: "Just tell the damn story."

Writing has become Ken's second life: he has been a Marine, played collegiate football, been a Texas wildcatter, cattle and horse rancher, professional film and TV actor and director, and now...a novelist. Who knew?

Ken Farmer's dialogue flows like a beautiful western river...it's the gold standard...Carole Beers
Web page: www.KenFarmer-Author.net

ISBN-13: - 978-1-7329119-6-3
ISBN-10: 1-7329119-6-7

Timber Creek Press
Imprint of Timber Creek Productions, LLC
312 N. Commerce St.
Gainesville, Texas 76240

Published by: Timber Creek Press
timbercreekpresss@yahoo.com
www.timbercreekpress.net
Twitter: @pagact
Facebook Book Page:
www.facebook.com/KenFarmerAuthor/
Ken's email: pagact@yahoo.com
214-533-4964

DEDICATION

This tome is book #16 in the award-winning, The Nations Series, #6 of the spin-off Bone Series and is dedicated to my beautiful grand daughters, Makena and Morgan Farmer.

ACKNOWLEDGMENT

The author gratefully acknowledges Lt. Colonel Clyde DeLoach, USMC (Ret.), Buck Stienke, Terry Heflin. retired English Professor at Tarrant County College, and award-winning, best-selling novelist Mary Deal for their invaluable help in proofing, beta reading and editing this novel.

This novel is a work of fiction...except the parts that aren't. Names, characters, places and incidents are either the products of the author's imagination or are used fictitiously and sometimes not. Any resemblance to actual persons, living or dead, business establishments, events or locales is entirely coincidental, except where they aren't.

TIMBER CREEK PRESS

PREFACE

BY KEN FARMER - AUTHOR

This story is a continuation of the adventures of Darrell Ulysses Bone and his wife, Loraine Rodriguez Bone, two modern day small town detectives trapped in 1899. It was told to me by Jethro Barthelomew Pereira, known to all his friends as just Padrino, a man of impeccable character.

He has chronicled all the adventures of Bone and Loraine to me and in this story...He tells of them meeting a beautiful detective with the

Pinkerton National Detective agency, named Silke Justice. Her full name was Silke Diane Justice. The name 'Silke' is a Germanic derivative from Latin, actually a form of Celia…meaning *'heavenly'* and Diane…meaning *'divine'*…It fits her.

She joins up with Bone and Loraine and legendary deputy US marshal, Bass Reeves, in chasing down the Big John Tackett gang—a vile, murderous bunch that had also killed Silke's mother and father in cold blood. The gang includes a criminal from 2019, well known to Bone and Loraine. They had arrested him for murder before they were flung back in time. How did he get there, too?

They get the unexpected answers to some of the age old questions physicists have asked since H.G. Wells about time travel.

You may choose to believe this story or not, it's up to you. I'm only presenting what I was told. I hope you enjoy the tale, find it interesting and maybe even informative.

§§§

CHAPTER ONE

FLYNN RANCH
1899

The shrill cry of a hunting Red Tailed Hawk pierced the morning quiet over the Broken Diamond F Ranch as he flew lazy circles above the adjacent prairie grass pasture on the other side of the creek

Ken Farmer

looking for his breakfast, a field mouse or perhaps a cottontail.

Bone and Loraine strolled hand-in-hand, along a game trail that bordered Black Creek.

He turned to her. "Baby, I may say stupid things, sometimes…I know I laugh when I'm not supposed to and don't when I am…Been told I'm three gallons of crazy in a two gallon bucket."

The year-round spring-fed waterway cut through Mason and Fiona Flynn's newly purchased full section of land that bordered Mason's sister, Mary Lou, and her husband Cletus Wilson's property in southwestern Cooke County, Texas.

The Wilsons had taken in *Annuna*, the diminutive *Anunnaki* alien who was stranded when her spacecraft crashed at Aurora, Texas, April 17, 1897. Fiona had named her *Lucy* so she could pose as an abandoned child. *

The *Anunnaki* look exactly like the denizens of Earth, but smaller—or it could be said that we look the same as the *Anunnaki*, only larger.

Detective Darrell Bone and Inspector Loraine Rodriguez had been accidentally transported back in time 120 years through an ancient Amerindian portal next to the present day lake, Possum

Kingdom, in Palo Pinto, County, Texas. It was several months earlier in October, 1898, during an electrical storm while they were taking refuge in a cave.

There were ancient petroglyphs carved into the side of the cave, including a circular spiral, thought by many to signify a portal to other dimensions, planets—or other times.

Bone and Loraine had since realized that after being partners with the Gainesville Police Department for four years from 2014 to 2018, they were actually in love.

They were married in December, 1898 in Gainesville in the back yard of Faye Skeans Boarding House.

The couple stopped to listen to the pleasant forest and creek sounds of cicadas, song birds, squirrels fussing up in the trees and frogs croaking.

Their eyes were drawn to a large mouth bass in the clear water of the creek, cruising along just under the surface, looking for a wayward insect or a minnow for a moment, before Bone continued.

"I know I'm a little crazy...or hell, maybe a lot crazy, and probably won't change...Love me or not. But, darlin', I guarantee that as long as I draw a breath, I love you and it's with a full heart…and you can carve that in stone."

The 5'3" Hispanic beauty turned and threw her arms about the 6'8" giant of man's neck and pulled him down to her face.

She kissed him on the lips with passion, that he returned with equal fervor, and then leaned back as her limpid brown eyes looked up into his amber gold ones. "My sweet Bone, you don't think I know that?…Do you remember what I said to you while I was sitting on your chest after I threw you over my head in Jacksboro…demonstrating some Kung Fu moves?"

He chuckled. "Pretty much. Kind of hard to forget…You said, you didn't want to wonder about me, you wanted to know what I was thinking every minute of the day like you wanted me know what you were thinking…"

Loraine interrupted him, "I said I liked open books, too…I love you, you big lug…I love your honesty…I love the fact that you can't ever hide anything from me…Does that answer your final question?"

He gave her his patented enigmatic grin. "Well, I just wanted to say it out loud."

She kissed him again. "And I love you for that, too...Just so you know, it doesn't matter to me if we stay here in this time frame or go back home to 2019...I'll love you wherever or whenever we are. You are part of my soul..." She looked past Bone through the trees toward the ranch road, twenty-five yards from the creek. "Who's that?"

Bone turned to see a man slumped in his saddle. His horse was slowly plodding toward the big two-story native rock house in the distance where Bone, Loraine and his godfather, Padrino, were staying with Bone's great grand parents, Sheriff Mason Flynn and Deputy US Marshal Fiona Miller Flynn, who was five months pregnant.

"That's Walt," Bone exclaimed. "He's hurt."

The two ran the short distance to the walking blue roan horse, slowing to a walk themselves so they wouldn't startle the animal.

Loraine grabbed the reins and stopped the horse. "Whoa, Blue, easy boy."

"He's been shot," said Bone as he eased the barely conscious long, lanky, ex-Texas Ranger, Walt Durbin, now the High Sheriff of Cooke County, out of the saddle and into his arms.

The coppery smell of fresh blood was strong as Bone gently laid him on the ground and pulled out a clean handkerchief from his parfleche.

"He's been shot in the chest. Doesn't look like it hit an artery or anything, but it's through and through," said Loraine as she took the hanky from Bone and pressed it to the wound under his shirt and vest, and then grabbed another from her own pocket.

Bone got Walt's blanket-covered canteen from where it was looped over the saddle horn of the Texas style, double-rigged saddle and held it to the Sheriff's lips. Walt took a little sip and looked up at the big man leaning over him.

"Fancy meetin' you here, Bone," he whispered weakly. "Just comin' to…see you."

"Who shot you, Walt?" asked Loraine.

"Bush…Bushwhacker."

"Do you know who it was?" inquired Bone.

Walt nodded. "B…Bank robber…He's from the future…" He passed out again.

Bone and Loraine exchanged glances…

* - *Legend of Aurora* - Published, May 30, 2014

Padrino sat on the wide front wraparound porch of the big native rock house built by the previous owners, Robert and Suellyn Manier, in a slat-back rocking chair having a glass of iced tea. The white-haired, seventy year old retired Master Gunnery Sergeant from the Marine Corps watched with interest, the blue roan horse slowly walking toward the house on the ranch road—and especially at the figure slumped over in the saddle.

Padrino had figured out how to transport himself from 2018 to 1898, with the help of an energy collecting crystal, formed from a large meteorite impact several millennia in the past, and his Zen meditation.

He came through the electromagnetic vortex in the same ancient Amerindian portal—the cave near Possum Kingdom Lake nearby in Palo Pinto County, to join Bone and Loraine.

He got to his feet when he saw Bone and Loraine exit the tree line that bordered Black Creek, run toward the shuffling horse, and Bone ease the man from the saddle to the ground.

"Uh-oh...Not good."

He set his glass on a small table next to his chair and made his way down the four steps of the stoop from the porch and headed, at a rapid walk, the four hundred yards between the house and the activity on the road.

"Got to get you some help…Pard, I'm going to carry him to the house and at least get the bleeding stopped…Jump on Blue and ride over next door to the Wilson's and get Lucy."

"Can do." She stuck her foot in the stirrup and swung up into the saddle. "Stirrups are too long, but no time to adjust them. I'll make do."

"That's my girl," said Bone as he picked Walt up like a child and headed toward the house with his long strides as if the 180 pound man weighed nothing.

Almost halfway to the house, he and Padrino came together.

"What's happened to Walt?" Padrino asked as they walked.

"Said he got bushwhacked by a bank robber…and get this…From the future."

"What?"

"Yep, that's what he said...'From the future'...before he passed out."

"Well, we shouldn't be surprised...We're here," commented Padrino.

"True enough."

"Wonder if it was from the same portal?" mused Padrino.

"I'm hoping Walt has some more information other than...*from the future*. That covers a lot of territory."

"Right. Could be our future or could be some other time all together.

Deputy US Marshal Fiona Miller Flynn met them at the gate in the white picket fence that surrounded the yard around the ranch house. She opened it for Bone and Padrino.

"He's not..."

"Not yet, but he's pretty weak...We need to stop the bleeding before Lucy gets here. Loraine rode over there on Walt's horse while we carried him up to the house. Where do you want me to lay him?" asked Bone.

"The guest bedroom to the left just past the front door. I'll go get it ready and fetch some towels and bandages." Fiona turned on her heel and moved as rapidly as her motherly condition warranted back up the steps and in the door.

Padrino opened the gingerbread screen door and then the front door for Bone to turn sideways and enter.

The door to the bedroom was already open and the covers pulled back on the four-poster bed inside.

Fiona walked rapidly back down the wide hallway to the bedroom, followed by her husband, Sheriff Mason Flynn.

Bone gently laid Walt on the bed while Fiona cut his bloody vest and collarless shirt away with her sewing scissors.

"Hand me a towel. Mason, go to the kitchen, I put some water on to heat. Fill a wash pan so I can clean him up…And bring some powdered alum from your saddlebags."

"Yes, dear," the dark-haired, broad shouldered lawman replied over his shoulder as he headed out the door.

"His breathing's getting pretty shallow, Bone," said Padrino.

"I know…See any sign of Loraine and Lucy?"

Padrino stepped to the front window. "As we speak…Cletus is pulling his buckboard up at the front with Lucy and Mary Lou. Loraine is already tying Blue to the hitching rail and loosening his girth."

"My bride made good time." Bone looked at his godfather. "Would you and Cletus mind unsaddlin' Blue and turning him out in the paddock? He's done his job for today."

"Good thought," replied Padrino as he headed out the door and down the walk, passing Lucy and Loraine hurrying their way in.

Mason was coming down the hallway with a pan of steaming water and bandages. Lucy let him enter first and followed right on his heels. Mason and Fiona's red and white border collie, Newton, was right behind.

He set the pan on the nightstand next to the bed for Fiona. She wasted no time in wetting one of the towels and gently wiping the blood away from Walt's chest.

"Fold up some of those bandages to make two pads," she directed as she took the alum from Mason, opened the small jar and sprinkled some of the white powder directly on Walt's wound on his

17

chest. Bone rolled him over on his side so she could reach the exit wound on his back to clean it and do the same procedure as the front.

Loraine folded the bandages into a four by four pads and placed one on top of the wound over the powder on his back, and then one on the front and held it tight while Fiona wrapped a long strip of cloth from a torn sheet around his body.

"Give it a minute or so for the alum and the pressure pads to work and then Lucy can do her thing," said Bone.

Lucy turned to Fiona. "I need your help like we did with Mason and again with Bone when they were shot."

"I understand," replied the statuesque raven-haired beauty. "It's still safe for my baby?"

Lucy nodded. "Yes, there's no problem up to about seven months." She walked around to the other side of the bed and laid down beside Walt on that side while Fiona laid on the near side. They joined hands over his body, nodded to each other and both closed their eyes.

Newton sat close beside the bed, close to his mistress, his head was cocked to one side.

In less than a minute, the familiar blue glow began to emanate first from Lucy, and then from Fiona. It got brighter and brighter almost filling the room, until the three on the bed could no longer be seen...

§§§

CHAPTER TWO

FLYNN RANCH HOUSE

Bone, Loraine, Mason, Cletus and Padrino were in the large back yard, playing a heated game of horseshoes while they waited for Lucy and Fiona to complete their ministrations to Walt.

They knew from past experiences that Lucy's technique of transferring healing life energy, similar to a blood transfusion, would take several hours. It could also take up to an additional hour for the donors to wake up following the procedure, as their own bodies regenerated.

Lucy had likened it to the story of *Chiron*, the wise Centaur who taught *Ascelepius*, the God of Medicine, the laying on of hands healing in Greek mythology. It was also the source of the *caduceus*, medicine's symbol of healing and the word, *Chi-ergy*, which evolved into surgery.

"That's six to zip," said Loraine as she pitched the draft-size horseshoe the forty feet to the box and watched it ring the steel stake with a clang.

Newton spun around in three circles, barking, and then sat down next to Loraine and looked up at her, and then at the others.

"Is there any way she could be cheating?" Bone asked Padrino.

"Not that I know of...unless she's mastered telekinesis..."

"Walt's awake," interrupted Mary Lou from the back door.

Mason glanced at Cletus as they all walked toward the door. "What'd he say?"

"Damn if I know," Cletus replied.

21

Bone looked over at the pair. "Magic."

"Huh?" they responded together as they followed the others inside with Newton on their heels.

The five horseshoe players entered the bedroom as Walt was carefully crawling over the still sleeping Fiona to get out of the bed on the room side. Lucy, on the other side, was also deep in slumber as she and Fiona recuperated—both wore peaceful expressions.

Newton reached out with his nose and sniffed of Fiona, and then looked up at Loraine.

"Let's just leave them alone to rest…It may be another hour," Loraine said softly. "…and go into the kitchen. Mary Lou has a fresh pot of coffee made…she also found one of Mason's shirts for you. Said he wouldn't mind…Be a little big on you." She handed it to Walt.

"Appreciate it." He pulled the blue twill cotton shirt on and buttoned the front.

He rubbed the spot on his chest where he took the round. "Huh, kinda sore…I know ya'll told me about what Lucy could do before. Didn't really believe it then…Do now." He glanced over at Bone.

"Don't feel bad, Sheriff, had trouble myself till she did it on me, too…and I had already died. Knew she could do it on birds and dogs…but me?" said Bone.

"Lucy must have a special path to God all mighty his self," commented Walt.

"She said we all can do it, we just haven't learned how," said Loraine. "I was able to do it to Bone a little back in our time and he returned the favor a couple of months ago when I got shot during an attempted stage holdup over in Jack County."

"Well, whatever, I'm much obliged an' I suspect my Frances Ann is also."

They entered the kitchen where Mary Lou was setting the last of the full cups of her hot coffee on the table.

"Anyone want cream and sugar? It's there on the table, too," she said.

"I need a big glass of water first, please, Ma'am…Got a powerful thirst."

"Oh yeah, meant to tell you about that," replied Mason. "Think I nearly drank the pitcher dry in that hotel room in Paradise after she healed me when I was shot in the back."

Newton crawled under the table and laid down with a grunt and a loud sigh.

Mary Lou set a quart Mason jar in front of him, filled with fresh well water. Walt picked it up and literally drained it in a little over a minute.

"My goodness, Sheriff…Do you need another?"

He grinned and handed her the jar. "Yessum, you don't mind."

She shook her head and filled it again from the red cast iron pitcher pump at the sink. "Got plenty."

"Thankee kindly, Miz Wilson."

"Oh, fiddle-faddle, call me, Mary Lou."

Walt nodded. "Yessum." He grinned and proceeded to down the second glass.

When he set the quart jar back on the table, Bone sat down in one of the chairs as did the others.

He took a sip from his cup, looked back up at Walt and asked, "Now, you said the guy that shot you was a bank robber and…from the future. Can you clarify that a little?"

Walt nodded again. "Well, yesterday afternoon, I got a call on that new telephony thing of that Bell feller we got in the office now…from the First State that they had just been robbed...Said the guy was 'bout thirty, dressed funny an' had a odd lookin' gun...Got thirty-thousand dollars...five thousand in gold Double Eagles."

"They say anything more about his funny outfit?" asked Loraine.

Walt shrugged. "Just he didn't wear no hat an' his hair was all spiky on top an' he wore a black, sorta tight fittin' short sleeve shirt with a picture of a camel an' the words *'Hump Day...Woo-hoo'* on it. Oh, the pants wadn't too odd, though...Just faded jeans, but wore out."

"What do you mean, 'wore out'?" asked Bone.

"Just that, they said they was holes in the knees an' up along the front of the leg an' a hole in the backside showin' he's wearin' some kind of yella underwear with red polkadots."

Bone and Loraine looked at one another and nodded.

"Hump-Day...that GEICO commercial," said Loraine.

"Wonder what kind of gun he had?" questioned Bone.

"Hell, I can tell you that. Saw it right up close...I was trackin' him out of town an' you know

Ken Farmer

that bald hill with the cedar trees on the west side, 'tween here an' Era?"

"Uh-huh," answered Bone.

"Well, as I rounded the hill…guess I was bein' real stupid an' wadn't watchin' up ahead, on account he stepped out from behind them bushes and pointed his gun right at me…It was like lookin' down the barrel of a cannon."

"What did it look like?" asked Loraine.

Walt raised his eyebrows. "Just like that one you an' Padrino carry."

She pulled her Kimber semiautomatic .45 from her holster in the middle of her back and held it up. "Like this?"

"Exactly." He nodded.

"It's another twelve years before the 1911 will be available…and then only to the military," said Padrino.

"Then the robber laughed and said, 'Okay, hell, thought it would be like in the movies…with a big posse on my tail, but it's just one hayseed sheriff…Who knew?'

"Last thing I remember was a big ball of fire an' somethin' whackin' me in the chest like a hammer…till I seen you."

"You musta been conscious enough to find your way here overnight."

"Don't remember nothin' till I looked up at Bone's face an' bein' kindly surprised...Then everthin' went black agin."

Bone grinned. "You said you were coming to see me, then passed out."

"Yep, then I woke up 'tween Fiona an' Lucy with my chest an' back a mite sore...Reckon I'm lucky that shot didn't knock me outta the saddle."

"I'd say," commented Mason.

"Think you can pick up the trail again?" asked Loraine.

"I 'spect...He didn't know much about hidin' his tracks. Just let me rest up a bit, still feelin' a mite pekid."

"No wonder...Looked like you lost a lot of blood," said Padrino. "Cletus and I cleaned the most of it off Blue and your saddle when we stripped your tack and turned him in the paddock with plenty of hay."

"Sure appreciate that, too. He took care of me."

"He's a goodun, for sure," added Mason.

Bone glanced at his wife, Loraine, and his godfather, Padrino. "Well, what do ya'll think?"

"His use of 'Okay' shows he's not from this time. That word doesn't become popular in the common vernacular until around 1930 or so…It's obvious he's from our time, give or take a year…."

Loraine picked up the thread, "That commercial he's referencing on his shirt first aired a few years ago and then they brought it back a month or so before we came here."

"What does Hump Day mean?" asked Walt.

"Started around 1965 or so and means Wednesday…the middle of the week," said Bone.

"If you make it to the middle, then you're over the hump," added Loraine. "It's downhill to the weekend."

Walt, Mason, Cletus and Mary Lou exchanged puzzled expressions and shrugs.

"It's like if we said 'clabber the milk' in our time, no one would know what we were talkin' about," commented Bone.

"Why?" asked Mary Lou.

"Uh, well, because the law says they have to pasteurize milk before they sell it to the public in our time," answered Loraine.

"Why?" Mary Lou inquired again.

"Never mind…Sorry we brought it up," said Bone. "Don't think it really matters much right now about how he got here, fact is…he's here."

"And we need to go find him," added Loraine. "Before he causes more mischief."

"I think committing armed robbery and attempting to kill a law officer is a bit more than cause mischief…If he has no qualms about shooting a lawman, he sure won't for anyone else," said Padrino.

"I think his bull dog attitude may have severely overloaded his hummingbird ass," offered Bone. "We've never failed to bring in some miscreant that we went after, have we, Pard?"

"Not yet."

Bone glanced at Loraine and Padrino. "What say we boogie over to that hill in the morning and pick up his trail?"

"If ya'll'l give me some time to get my legs under me, I'll go with you."

"That's all right, Walt, this dirt bag is one of the kind of thugs we rousted regularly in our time. We know his type."

"But, it's my responsibility. He robbed a bank in my county."

Ken Farmer

"It's going to take several days for you to build back all that blood you lost…besides we're living in the county now, you can deputize us and let us do our thing," said Loraine.

"This goes against my grain…"

"But, they're right, Walt," said Lucy as she and Fiona walked in the room. "We need some water and do you have any coffee left?"

"It's a yes to both," said Mary Lou. "Sorry for taking over your kitchen, Fiona. Didn't want to disturb you."

"You know you can use my kitchen any time, sister-in-law." Fiona grinned and gave Mary Lou a hug from the back as she was getting glasses from the cupboard for their water.

"Any idea where he was heading, Walt?" asked Bone as Lucy and Fiona guzzled their water.

"Not really, Bone."

"Guess we'll go where he takes us, but he was kind of heading in the direction of the cave down on the Brazos, wasn't he?" postulated Bone.

"Maybe he did come in that way and is trying to get back," suggested Padrino.

"Any thing special about the tracks of the horse he was riding?"

"Now that you mention it, Bone, yeah. The back feet are kindly straight and narrow...like a mule's hoof," replied Walt. "Front's purty normal."

"I say let's head in the direction of Valley View and try to cut his sign."

"Pulling a Bass Reeves trick, huh, hon?"

"Can't think of anybody any better." Bone grinned.

"Couldn't have said it better myself," said Fiona. "He made me feel like Ned in *McGuffey's First Reader*...His long time partner, Marshal Jack McGann, used to say that Bass could track a fish up a river."

§§§

CHAPTER THREE

FLYNN RANCH
COOKE COUNTY, TEXAS

Mason finished loading the panniers on Bart, the bay pack horse, tied to the hitching rail in front of the house.

Bone's black half-Friesian, seventeen hand gelding, Hildebrandt, Loraine's sorrel mare, Sweet

Face and Padrino's claybank gelding, Star, were already tacked up and tied to the rail.

"Ya'll sure you don't want me to go?" asked Mason.

"It's all right, you got your hands full here gettin' your new place to the way you want it…Fiona doesn't need to be out working the cattle and such at her stage," replied Bone.

"Besides, this is what we do," added Loraine. "It's entirely possible we've handled this scumbag before."

"Hey, good, Pard. Didn't think of that one. If he's from the Gainesville area, there's a damn good chance." Bone paused a moment. "That description does sound kinda like a ne'er-do-well we've seen down at the Governor's Lounge a time or two."

"What's the Governor's Lounge?" asked Fiona.

"Local saloon…call them clubs in our time…Cop hang out," said Loraine.

"Most of us were regulars after our shift was over. Busted more than one we saw in there," added Bone, then he turned to Loraine. "Say, you remember that gay guy we busted for killin' his boyfriend in Peach's house with one of her butcher knives, and then putting the body next to her while she was asleep?"

"Uh-huh, she had taken one of my sleeping pills and didn't know anything until the next morning when she woke up next to a stiff...His name was Lenny Taylor, wasn't it?"

"An IT tech for the city...A real electronics whiz," said Bone.

"What's gay?...You mean happy?" asked Mason.

Loraine looked at him and shook her head. "In our time it's what many homosexuals call themselves."

"Richard von Krafft-Ebing referred to it as Sexual Inversion," said Fiona.

"Oh, queer," added Mason. "A Nancy.'

Bone nodded. "Close enough. He was pissed at his boyfriend, Joe, for hitting on Peach at the Governor's Lounge...Planted an electronic tracking device on him and followed him, when he broke into Peach's house...and then knifed him in the back when he saw him smell her panties in her bedroom while she was passed out."

"So, she wakes up next to the body in her bed and everyone thinks she did it," said Fiona.

"Right," responded Loraine.

"How'd you catch him?" asked Mason.

"Like I said, he was an electronics whiz with the city and had added a remote microscope lens that could be hooked up to a computer monitor."

"Bone found a white cotton fiber in the wooden handle of the butcher knife in Joe's back that matched the white cotton gloves Lenny always wore when he worked with electronics so he wouldn't leave body oils," added Loraine.

"Let's see if we can get hold of Peach. Maybe they're at the ranch close to the statue. She would know anything there is to know about Lenny Taylor. He got twenty-to life down at Huntsville as I recall," commented Bone.

"Ya'll are just way too complicated in your time…electronic trackin' things, computers an' God only knows what all."

"Sometimes I think you're right, Mason," said Bone as he took out his Galaxy and hit Peach's number. "One reason why we like it here…Hold that crystal of yours close, Padrino."

His godfather stepped closer and removed the unique *moldivite* energy crystal from his BDU pocket.

He put his phone on speaker and heard it ring two and then three times, then, "Bone, Bone, Bone, Bone, it's you?"

"Just a minute, Peach, let me check...Dang, what do you know, it's me all right."

"Bless your heart...What's hap'nin'?" replied the tall Georgia native, brunette, forensics technician for the Gainesville Police Department.

"Need you to find out something for us."

"Honey, if I don't know it, you can bet your sweet bootie I can find it...You know I'm your huckleberry."

"Right...You remember that Lenny Taylor fellow that planted Joe's body in your bed?"

"Oh, sweet pea, I've been tryin' so hard to forget that and here you go bringin' it back up. Can't tell you how much I appreciate it...You're lucky you're not here so I can put some more of my special purgative in your coffee again."

"Ooh, talk about bad memories."

"Interestin' you brought Mister Taylor up."

"How so?"

"Bone...Stella here, I'm working on his case now." The five-two blond bombshell police Investigator leaned close to Peach's phone.

"Hey, Stella...what do you mean, working on his case now?...Thought they sent him down to the pen."

"Never made it. He escaped over a week ago, then he goes down and robs the First State, and then disappears. I mean vanished from sight...Can't find hide nor hair of him."

"I can help you out on that, little bit...He's here..."

"He's there? Get out! But, how?..."

"Damn if I know, but he apparently is, according to the description we got...He pulled the same stunt at the First State, and then shot Sheriff Durbin, yesterday."

"Is the sheriff all right?"

"Yeah, thanks to Lucy...We're fixing to go after him. Anything in his jacket about where he was from before he came to Gainesville?"

"Have to get back to you on that Bone, when we get to the station...his file's on my desk. You'll have to wait till we come back out here to your ranch close to that statue with its power ruby, for me to call," said Stella.

"That's fine...He got hold of a 1911A somehow and used it on the sheriff," added Loraine.

"Can answer that, too. It was the duty officer's sidearm back in the jail. Taylor hit him over the head with his food tray and took his weapon and his two backup mags."

"I've told 'em to go to plastic or Bakelite trays instead of metal," said Bone. "And what the sam hill was the duty officer doing wearing his sidearm back in the lockup?"

"Don't know…Dumb move, alright," said Stella.

"Ya'll watch him, hear? He's slicker'n a pocket full of puddin'," commented Peach.

"Yeah, I remember," said Bone. "Laterbye." He hit the red phone icon to terminate the call.

"I remember that little worm," commented Loraine.

"Me too, but he's a smart little worm," replied Bone as he swung up into the saddle. "But, here in this time frame, he doesn't have access to his electronics or energy sources like our crystal."

"Ya'll take care, Bone," said Lucy.

"You know me."

"That's why I said it," the diminutive alien replied.

"When do you think you'll be back?" asked Mason.

"When we get him," answered Loraine.

"Got enough ammo?" Fiona inquired.

Bone grinned. "You know there's no such thing as enough ammo, grandma,"

"You best get on out of here before I have to hurt you," Fiona replied with a smile. "Keep him in line, Padrino," she added.

"I'll just sic Loraine on him," the white-haired retired Marine said as he turned his horse and trotted after Bone and Loraine.

"Wonder if that guy knows how much trouble he's in?" mused Mason.

"Probably not," answered Lucy as she and the others headed back toward the house.

Loraine looked over at Bone as the three trotted down the ranch road to the entrance. "How far is it to Valley View?"

"About ten miles, but if we don't cut his tracks around five miles out, we'll have to go up to where he shot Walt and try to pick up his trail...We can make around eight miles an hour at a road trot, so if we don't find anything in forty-five minutes, we guessed wrong...Keep your eyes peeled for those narrow back feet."

"Need to pick up his trail by dark…so we can get a general direction on where he's going," said Padrino.

"That would be a start," added Loraine. "It's a good thing Fiona deputized us as deputy marshals in case we have to leave Cooke County."

Padrino nodded. "You think?"

MARYSVILLE, TEXAS

Eight men rode up to the Miller Justice ranch outside of Marysville in northern Cooke County.

The well-kept, white painted clapboard, three bedroom ranch house was almost a quarter mile off the wagon road that led southeast to St. Jo and was adjacent to the Gunter Ranch.

The Marysville area was a popular staging location for cattle drives in the post civil war era. Cattlemen from north Texas would gather their herds here and then head north and west to join up with the Chisholm Trail after crossing the Red River at Sivells Bend.

Miller Justice stepped out of his house and walked to the fence in front. He carried a twelve gauge double barreled shotgun loosely in his right hand. His wife, Mae Ellen, came out the door and stood on the porch, twisting a dishtowel in her hands. A six year old, towheaded boy was holding on to her dress at her side.

"What can I do for you fellers?"

"Needin' some water and some fresh mounts," said the leader, Big John Tackett.

"Got plenty water, help yourselves over to the trough at the barn yonder. Ain't got any horses for sale, though."

"Well, much obliged fer the water…but never said nothin' 'bout buyin' 'em."

The men behind Tackett chuckled.

Justice started to raise his shotgun to his hip, but, he never made it as four of the men drew and fired on him. All four rounds struck home.

Mae Ellen screamed and ran down the steps toward her already dead husband on the walkway and three of the men shot her before she ever got to Miller.

The little boy screamed and ran back inside the house.

"Git the kid," said Big John. "An' fire the house."

Two of the men dismounted and ran inside while the others rode over to the barn to get what horses they could and water the rest.

They pulled rein in front of the water trough and the rest dismounted.

The two that ran into the house joined the others.

"Take care of the kid?" asked Big John.

One of the men, Bull Weatherly, grinned and nodded. "Said to, didn't ya?"

An oddly dressed young man stepped out of the big open double doors to the barn, both his hands were high above his head.

Big John and two of the gang drew their sidearms.

"Hey, hey, just a minute, I'm on the lam."

"What's 'on the lam'?" asked Tackett.

"Runnin' from the law."

"For what, dressin' funny?" asked Big John as he and the others laughed.

"I killed the Gainesville sheriff."

"You killed Walt Durbin?"

"If that was the sheriff, yeah, drilled him in the center of his chest."

"Why was he after you?" asked Tackett.

"Robbed the First State."

"Well, might could use you…Got a horse?"

"Tied around back, I was just hiding out in this barn till night."

"Got a name?" asked Big John.

"Taylor, Lenny Taylor."

§§§

CHAPTER FOUR

COOKE COUNTY

Bone held up his hand as he pulled rein on Hildebrandt. "Well, we're substantially past the line he would have taken to the Brazos…must have gone another direction." He shrugged. "Back toward Era and that hill."

The threesome reined around and headed north and west toward the hill where Walt was shot.

Thirty minutes later they rode up to the bald hill with the copse of cedar on the west side.

"Ya'll wait here," Bone said as they stopped a little short of the road from Era toward the ranch. "No need in adding a bunch more tracks till I locate the ones we're looking for."

He nudged Hildebrandt up to the grove of trees and located an area on the back side with several piles of horse apples no more than two days old. The ground was fairly well pounded down.

"Waited here for a couple hours," Bone muttered.

He quickly spotted the unique rear hoof prints and followed them down to the road, turned west and followed them to a T road from the north.

"Okay, this way, headed north," Bone yelled back at Loraine and Padrino leading the pack horse.

Padrino stopped when they got down to the road from where they were waiting and dismounted. He bent over, picked up something from the road, slipped it in his jacket pocket, remounted and he and Loraine trotted over to catch up with Bone.

Padrino removed the item from his pocket when they were beside Bone and handed it to him.

".45 caliber ACP brass." He held it up in front of his face. "Yep, figured that's what you were picking up."

"Never know if you might need it for evidence," Padrino replied as they trotted off to the north on the little-used ranch road.

"Where do you think he's heading?" asked Loraine.

"Well, we're right in the middle of what the natives of Cooke County called the Chisum Trail, not to be confused with the Chisholm Trail. This one was founded by John Chisum...Heads north to join up with the Chisholm Trail the other side of Ringling, Chickasaw Nation or west to Fort Sumner, New Mexico."

"John Wayne played him in the movie, *Chisum*, in 1970...Billy the Kid worked for Chisum in New Mexico," said Padrino. "AKA Brushy Bill Roberts."

"And Chisum moved to New Mexico from Cooke County in 1866...Lived down around

Bolivar near Valley View...Lots of folks confuse Jessie B. Chisholm's Trail with John Chisum's Western Trail, but Jessie B. Chisholm's Trail doesn't really begin until the north side of the Red," commented Bone.

"How do you know all that stuff?" asked Loraine.

He grinned and squeezed Hildebrandt up into a road trot. "It's a gift."

"Damn you, Bone," Loraine bumped Sweet Face up alongside him to swing her hand at the back of his head—he ducked, but she knocked his dark green John Bull hat from his head to the dusty road.

MARYSVILLE, TEXAS

There were just a few tendrils of smoke drifting up from the still smoldering embers of what was formerly the Miller Justice ranch.

The doors to the barn and the adjacent coral gate stood open in mute testimony of their present empty state.

A lone rider on a line-back dun was trotting toward the Justice ranch when they reined the horse to a stop for a moment, and then spurred the animal to a hard gallop in the direction of the smoke.

The rider pulled the well-muscled Quarterhorse into a sliding stop. The gelding's back feet drew a long set of parallel lines in the dirt that looked like the number 11, with his haunches brushing the ground, as the person astride him did a running dismount well before the animal stopped.

The female rider stumbled to her knees at the body of the man on the walkway and checked for life signs. She found none, got back to her feet and scrambled over to the woman, only a few feet away and felt her pulse—she was also dead.

The twenty-three year-old strawberry blond young lady slumped down on her knees and unabashedly sobbed, her reddish blond tresses, in a long, thick, single braid, draped over her left shoulder. "Oh, Mama…Mama…"

Her trim body shook with emotion for a moment, and then her head jerked up, and she looked around the yard.

She jumped to her feet, spun in a circle and ran toward the barn, screaming, "Billy, Billy!" The woman turned, walking backward and continued calling, "Billy, where are you?"

She ran back over to the still hot embers of the house and studied the collapsed pile of mostly burned timbers, the still standing native stone chimney, and the iron wood stove where the kitchen once was as best she could, searching for any sign of the body of her six year old brother.

The distraught woman dropped to her knees again, reached inside her denim jacket, pulled out a handkerchief, dried her eyes somewhat and blew her nose.

She got to her feet walked back to the still standing green three plank fence and carefully searched the ground outside, counting the horse tracks.

"Eight," she hissed. "It took eight of the bastards to kill my family." She looked up at the sky. "God as my witness…The murdering sons of bitches are gonna pay. If it takes the rest of my life…They're gonna pay."

She was interrupted by the sound of hoofbeats coming from the south in the direction of Myra. Her hand was a blur as she slicked her ivory-gripped Colt .38-40 Peacemaker from the reverse grip holster on her shapely left hip.

The attractive woman pulled her dusty, sweat-stained gray Stetson down to shade her eyes from the afternoon sun and stood facing the three riders with her feet apart and her Colt held at her hip, pointed in their direction.

"Who the hell are you?" she snapped as Bone, Loraine and Padrino reined their mounts to a halt.

"Whoa, easy there, girl. I'm Cooke County Deputy Sheriff Bone, this is my wife, Deputy Sheriff Loraine Bone and my godfather, Padrino." He pulled his coat back to show his badge. "What's happened here?"

Her shoulders slumped as some of the tension left her body, and she lowered the muzzle of her shooter.

"Someone has murdered my mother and father…Counted eight sets of tracks…I can't find my little brother…or his body."

Loraine dismounted first and stepped over to comfort the younger woman. She put her arms around her and pulled her close. That was all it took to open the flood gates.

Her body racked with sobs as she jerked, trying to get her breath.

"Let it all out, honey, let it go," Loraine said softly to her as she held her tightly.

Bone and Padrino dismounted and led the horses, including the girl's line-back dun, over to the water trough while Loraine tended to the distressed young woman.

"Looks like Lenny has joined up with this group of animals," said Bone as he scoped out the tracks in front of the barn while the horses were drinking.

Padrino nodded. "That makes nine."

"Just about even, then, I'd say," replied Bone as he and Padrino walked back over to the two women.

"Do you have any idea who they were?" Loraine asked as Bone and Padrino walked up.

She shook her head. "Not really…Have heard rumors of a gang run by a Big John Tackett that's been on a tear over in Arkansas and east Texas, but I don't really know…or care for that matter. I intend on huntin' them down…whoever they are."

"Why don't you let us handle it Miss, it's what we do. The man we're following seems to have joined up with them," said Bone.

She looked up at Bone with her flinty sky-blue eyes for a long moment, and then reached in her front jacket pocket, pulled out a badge and handed it to the big man.

Bone looked down at the thick brass shield in his hand that had PINKERTON NATIONAL DETECTIVE AGENCY engraved on the face. He showed it to Loraine and Padrino.

"And you would be?" asked Bone.

"Justice…Silke Justice, Detective. This was my family's ranch…I just came for a visit." She reached out and took her proffered badge back from Bone. "Now, who is this man you're trackin'?"

"One Lenny Taylor. He robbed the First State in Gainesville day before yesterday and shot the sheriff in the chest…"

"He killed Walt?" she asked.

"Didn't say that. He's managed to pull through…" Bone looked questioningly at Loraine and Padrino.

"Just as well tell her, Bone, looks like we're going to be riding together.

"Tell me what, ya'll?" Silke asked.

"Well, what say we all go yonder under that big live oak and sit at your picnic table…this may take a little explaining."

Her brow wrinkled in confusion. "You say so." She turned and led the way.

They took seats on benches either side of the cedar plank table.

"Well, let's have it," said Silke. "Trail's gettin' cold."

Bone looked at Loraine and Padrino, took a breath and started, "We're not from this time."

Silke frowned. "What do you mean, 'not from this time'?"

"We're...uh, Well, we're from the future."

Silke looked at Bone, then at Padrino and finally at Loraine. "You're from the future?...As in...?"

"2019," said Loraine.

Silke raised one of her eyebrows. "That's a hundred and twenty years from now."

"Correct...Several months ago, in our time, Bone took me fishing...we weren't married then...to Possum Kingdom Lake down in Palo Pinto County. A freak storm came up and we took refuge in an old cave. Noticed there were ancient Indian petroglyphs carved in the walls...One was this large spiral..."

"Like Loraine said, we took refuge from the storm and right after we got inside, a big bolt of lightning hit the top of the hill…Kinda made our skin tingle, but we didn't think much of it at the time except that we were lucky to get into the cave when we did."

Loraine picked the story back up. "So, the storm included rain, and then a real heavy fog and when it cleared off, we stepped back out…"

"And the lake was gone…" interrupted Bone with his enigmatic grin. "So was my car, uh automobile…Wasn't anything there, but the Brazos River down in the canyon…that I'm sure you're familiar with."

"In our time, we're cops with the Gainesville Police Department. Bone is a Detective and I'm an Inspector…we've been partners for four years…After we were here in this time period a couple of months or so, we found out we were in love and got married in Gainesville in November." She looked over at Bone and they exchanged winks.

Padrino jumped in, "Seems that cave is an ancient Amerindian sacred portal. Legends have it that the spiral petroglyph is a sign that it's located on what is known as a magnetic ley line and under certain circumstances, like a lightning strike, or certain phases of the moon, an electromagnetic vortex can form and whoever happens to be inside is sent to another time."

Silke looked at Loraine, and then Bone. "What did he just say?"

"He said it was magic," replied Bone.

Loraine grinned. "The human race has referred to anything they don't understand in the physical world as 'magic', for a couple thousand years."

"I can agree with that," said Silke. "You said that Walt pulled through from being shot in the chest and that was just yesterday…What are you not telling me?"

They exchanged glances again.

"You remember a newspaper article in the Dallas Morning News on April 19, 1897 about a spacecraft that crashed at Aurora, Texas?" asked Bone.

Silke nodded. "Read about it…Paper said they buried the pilot in the local cemetery and that he was not of this world."

"There was a survivor," said Loraine.

§§§

CHAPTER FIVE

RED RIVER

Big John Tackett turned in his saddle to address the gang, "Awright, listen up, we're all gonna follow Comanche Bob, single file, across the river. This is one of the places where they took cattle herds across, but that was near thirty year ago...This here crossin' at Sivells Bend is fair shallow this time of year, but notorious for quicksand...River's changed course twicet since then...so don't git out of the line. I ain't goin' after you...Clear?"

Big John nodded at Comanche Bob to lead out. He followed behind the half-breed about two lengths. The others trailed behind him at the same spacing.

The water crept up to the horse's bellies and just a bit past. Most of the men took their feet out of their stirrups and rested them forward on the horse's shoulders to keep their boots from getting wet. They crossed the main channel, rode up on a sandbar in the middle, then across another side channel.

The river was only a little over a hundred yards wide at this point in the bend—one reason the cattlemen used it in days gone by.

One by one, the horses climbcd up thc sandy bank on the north side and gathered. Several shook violently to get rid of the dripping water, waiting on the last to cross—Lenny Taylor.

Fear was written on his face in bold type. His eyes were big as saucers as he constantly changed his view of the reddish, muddy, slow-moving water, from side to side. He didn't have to worry as his stolen horse was going to follow the others anyway.

His grulla gelding lunged the last couple of yards through the water to gain purchase on the thirty degree bank up to the others, almost dumping Lenny. He grabbed the saddlehorn with a death grip, from both hands.

"What in hell you scared of, Taylor?" asked Big John.

"Can't swim."

"Don't much think you can drown in three feet of water, lessen you try to walk across on yer hands."

The other men laughed at the greenhorn.

"We'll pitch camp up yonder next to Walnut Bayou where that sharp horseshoe is…Got water on three sides…Let's ride."

MILLER RANCH

Bone, Loraine, Padrino, and Silke finished digging side-by-side graves for Silke's mother and father over on a small knoll near where the house once stood.

"Mama loved to come up here and picnic when the weather was nice," Silke said as she wiped the tears from her eyes with the back of her hands.

She turned to the others. "If ya'll don't mind, I'd like to look for my baby brother some more."

Bone nodded. "Lets scatter so we can cover more ground."

The others agreed. He and Silke took the wooded area on the side of the homeplace and the back, Loraine headed toward the barn. Padrino was giving the embers and remains of the house another going over since they had cooled quite a bit.

Silke worked her way down to the small creek that ran along the west side of the property and combed through the brush along the banks.

Loraine searched through the barn, climbing up to the loft in the hopes the child had crawled up there to hide from the devastation below.

Forty-five minutes later, Bone, Silke and Loraine gathered out in front of the burned-out remains of the house. Each shook their head to indicate no sign at all of Billy.

They all turned as one to see Padrino walking toward them from the area behind the house. He was carrying a wet, limp, form in his arms. Tears were running down his face.

Silke dropped to her knees with a heart-rending scream as Padrino brought her brother's body to her.

"Oh, Billy, Billy…" was all she could get out before her emotion closed her voice with sobs.

"He was down in the well. I think he climbed down the well rope to hide and couldn't get back up…He was still holding on to the rope when I looked down and saw him…I'm so sorry, Silke…God knows my heart hurts for you."

Bone stepped over to Padrino. "Give him to me," he said softly as he reached out his arms.

He took the young boy's cold body and held it tightly to his chest, slowly sank to his knees and closed his eyes.

Padrino and Loraine exchanged glances as Silke got to her feet with a puzzled expression.

They watched as a soft blue glow began to effuse from Bone and envelope him and Billy. It grew brighter and brighter until it was almost hard to look at.

Silke looked at Padrino and Loraine, crossed her arms, held them close to her bosom and said reverently, sotto voce, "The laying on of hands...Praise God."

The glow eventually began to lose some of its intensity as Bone continued to hold Billy close to his chest with his head bowed over him.

The blue finally dispersed and Bone slowly raised his head. His massive hand was cupped behind Billy's head holding it also close to his chest. He took a deep breath, looked down and noticed a slight twitch in the child's eye lids.

Silke had a sharp intake of air as she brought her right hand to her mouth and tears rolled down her cheeks. She stepped forward as Bone rose shakily to his feet and handed her baby brother to her.

He slumped back down like his legs had turned to rubber, as Loraine ran to her husband, knelt beside Bone, and held him to her to keep him from falling over in exhaustion.

She looked at Padrino. "Bring the canteens, he and Billy both will need them...Breathe, Baby, breathe...Big breaths."

Bone followed her directions, breathing deep, yoga style.

Billy stirred, opened his eyes and blinked a couple of times. "Sissy?…Why are you cryin'?"

"Because I'm happy, honey…We found you."

"Oh, right." He nodded and looked around a little. "One of the bad men found me in the house and brought me out to the well. He looked around and said for me to climb down the well rope an' be quiet…I'm really thirsty."

Padrino handed him one of the canteens and he drank several deep draughts and then looked back up at Silke.

"When I didn't hear no more sounds…I tried to climb back up the rope, but I couldn't, so I just held on…All I remember is gettin' so cold…an' then I looked up an' saw you."

Tears started to flow down his cheeks. "I love you, Sissy…Thank you." He snuggled his head against her breasts.

Bone finally raised his head and reached for the proffered open canteen from Padrino and proceeded to drain it.

He looked at Loraine. "Wow, that was amazing…I guess when I did it when you were shot, kinda opened the gates…I was completely aware of everything when I was passing that healing energy to you, but this time, everything disappeared, except for the blue light."

"Lucy said we could all do it, we just hadn't learned how...Must be a matter of focus."

"And need," added Padrino.

Bone nodded and got to his feet with Loraine holding on to his arm. "Huh...Weak as a kitten."

"It will pass," said Padrino. "The cold water must have helped keep Billy at a point that you could revive him...They released a movie just before I transported here about a boy that fell through the ice on a lake...was under for about fifteen minutes and had no pulse for forty-five...and then came back...Think it's called *Breakthrough*."

"In more ways than one," commented Loraine. "I think God had a whole lot to do with it and this."

"Amen...No way could have done it by myself," said Bone.

"Another reason we're here, I surmise," added Padrino. "There was a very famous judge by the name of William Wayne Justice born in Texas in 1920..."

They looked at one another.

"Could be," said Bone as he stepped over to Silke and Billy.

"How're you feeling, Pard?"

"Hungry." He looked up at Silke. "Momma an' Daddy?"

She slowly shook her head.

He nodded somberly. "Saw the bad men shoot Papa an' then Mama...an' I ran. Should stayed an' fought 'em," Billy said as he began to tear up again.

"No, baby, you did right. There was too many of them," his sister said as the group walked toward the horses still over by the barn.

"Looks like the gang's headed north toward Sivells Bend and the Chickasaw Nation," said Bone as he looked at the tracks.

"Good thing Fiona deputized us," commented Loraine.

"Fiona? Deputy US Marshal Fiona Miller Flynn?"

"One and the same," replied Bone.

"She's my idol, my inspiration to get into law enforcement," commented Silke.

"She's my great-grandmother," said Bone.

"Excuse me?"

"Like we said, we're from 2019, and we found out when we got here that she and the sheriff were Bone's great grandparents...We helped her and her husband, Sheriff Mason Flynn, on a kidnapping and horse rustling case...Bone took a bullet meant for her and actually died. If he hadn't and Fiona was killed...Well, Bone would just cease to exist," commented Loraine. "That's where that survivor of the spacecraft crash we mentioned is involved."

"My goodness, not sure I can handle all this at one time," Silke responded.

They stripped the tack from the horses and turned them into the paddock beside the barn with plenty of hay and built a fire pit over under the tree by the picnic table.

"Now, you want to tell me about that survivor?" asked Silke as she helped Loraine prepare supper for them.

"Well, it seems the aliens, known as the *Anunnaki*, have been visiting Earth for many thousands of years. They're also known as the *Watchers*...She and her mate were in a pitched battle in outer space with some other, rather malevolent, aliens bent on conquering our planet...Her craft was damaged and crashed at

Aurora, Texas on April, 17, 1897, as that newspaper article said."

Bone walked up with an armload of deadwood for the fire, dropped it next to the pit and picked up Loraine's story.

"She and Mason discovered her and because she was so close in looks and size to an Earth child, they named her Lucy. Then they took her to Mason's sister and her husband...Mary Lou and Cletus adopted Lucy, pretending she was an abandoned, mute child to hide her...Loraine, Padrino, and I met Lucy in 2014 and helped her get rescued by her people after one hundred and seventeen years*...She taught us about the energy healing." *Legend of Aurora* - 2014

"Lucy brought Mason back to life after he had died from being shot in the back...brought Bone back...he had also died from taking that round meant for Fiona, as I mentioned earlier, and then saved Sheriff Durbin, yesterday," added Loraine.

Silke smiled and nodded. "Like I said...God's work."

§§§

CHAPTER SIX

WALNUT BAYOU

It was well past gloaming as the Tackett gang was having their coffee after supper. They had banked the fire by digging a two-foot deep hole and piling the dirt in a berm around it. The berm and the surrounding woods blocked most of the light from being seen at a distance.

"That's an interestin' shooter you got there, Taylor, where'd you git it?" asked Big John.

"Stole it, along with the horse when I broke out of jail."

"Lemme see it," demanded the leader.

Lenny pulled the Colt 1911A from his waist band and handed it to the large man. "Careful, there's one in the chamber."

"How's it work?"

"There's seven .45 caliber rounds in the handle and one in the chamber, like I said. At this stage, all you have to do is pull the hammer back till it locks, point it and squeeze the trigger."

"How do you put another bullet in the chamber? It ain't got no cylinder," commented one of the gang members, Whitey Copeland, an albino.

"Like I said, there's seven in the handle and when the one in the chamber is fired, the weapon automatically racks back, pulls the top bullet from the stack, shoves it into the chamber and cocks the hammer at the same time…Just squeeze the trigger again. It'll shoot as fast as you can pull the trigger."

"You're funnin' us," said one of the others, Duce Walton.

"Kid you not. It's called a semiautomatic handgun…Uh…It's an experimental model the deputy I took it from was carrying."

"Does it take regular .45 bullets?" asked Big John.

"Uh, no…That's kind of the problem, the bullets are experimental, too. The shells you use in your Colt revolvers have a thicker rim and won't fit in this weapon."

"What are you gonna do for bullets?" asked J.R. Duncan.

"I got two magazines from the deputy and counting the ones left in the gun…That's it."

"What were you in jail for?" asked Big John.

"Killed a guy."

"What'd he do?" asked J.R.

"He…uh…Betrayed me and I put a knife in his ribs."

"Don't have much of a conscience, do you?" stated Bull Weatherly.

"Not when it comes to betrayal," answered Lenny.

"Show us how it works…Shoot two rounds at that oak tree over yonder," commented Whitey.

Tackett handed him the weapon, Lenny thumbed the hammer back and aimed at the twelve inch white oak on the other side of camp, about forty feet—he squeezed the trigger twice. The double roar sounded almost like one shot.

There were two chunks of bark about the size of a silver dollar that exploded from the tree. The brass kicked out to the side, hitting the ground just after the bullets hit the tree.

"Damnation!" exclaimed J.R.

"Feller could shoot up a lot of ammunition in a hurry with that thing," said Duce.

"Could have the effect of scarin' the piss out of somebody too…Shoots faster than a Gatling Gun…We'll have to get you another shooter, so's you can save that one for…uh, emergencies…or somethin'," said Tackett.

JUSTICE RANCH

"Silke…interesting name…Short for something? Or a nickname?" asked Bone.

She smiled and snuggled Billy closer to her, and then took a sip of the stout trail brew Loraine had made. "No, it's a Germanic derivative from Latin, actually a form of Celia...meaning 'heavenly'...My mother was a school teacher...Taught Latin and French, among other things. She loved the name, so I got it, along with my middle name, Diane...meaning 'divine'...Silke Diane Justice."

"Heavenly Divine Justice." Loraine smiled, "Looks like they had high expectations of you."

"Must have been tough trying to live up to your names," commented Padrino.

"Not really, I have high expectations of myself...regardless of my names. Guess that's why I was so driven to be in law enforcement, especially after I read about Marshal Fiona Miller Flynn...Can still remember...must have been around fourteen or fifteen...that newspaper article that described her, 'as a dashing brunette of charming manners, expert shot and a superb horsewoman...and brave to the verge of recklessness'." She grinned. "Tried to become a Deputy US Marshal, but they said I was too young and needed experience...so I went to work for the Pinkertons."

"What type work have you been doing?" asked Bone.

"Undercover...and been hired out to track bank robbers and wanted outlaws...Rather odd since it's about the same thing I'd be doin' as a Deputy US Marshal...It's good experience, though."

"When did you go to work for the Pinkertons?" inquired Loraine.

"When I was twenty...three years ago."

Bone flashed his enigmatic grin. "Well, Silke Diane, you may fit in with us just fine. Who knows, maybe you'll get to meet Bass Reeves."

"Ya'll know Bass Reeves?" Silke exclaimed, sitting up slightly.

"Worked with him, Brushy Bill Roberts, Jack McGann and Selden Lindsey, several times...Not counting Fiona and Mason, of course," commented Bone.

"Bass gave me away at our wedding..." said Loraine with a big grin. "...and Fiona was my Matron of Honor."

"Oh, my goodness, I'm gettin' a head rush." She waved her hand in front of her face.

"I'm assuming you can use that shooter on your hip?" said Bone.

"I can. Show you tomorrow, if you like."

"Sounds good...Bass is partial to the .38-40 Peacemakers, also. Carries two...in reverse draw, plus a .41 cal Colt birdshead in a shoulder holster," commented Loraine.

"Bass likes .38-40? I would have thought he'd carry a .44 or .45," Silke replied.

"Tried...Judge Parker gave him one as a gift one time that he carried for a year...said he didn't like it and went back to his .38-40s. He's ambidextrous, you know," said Bone.

"No I didn't. How unusual...Most men like more knock down power."

"Bass's response to that is it's all about where you put the bullet."

"Oh, that's true...Two, or one for that matter, to the forehead will drop anyone, whereas two to the chest, even with a .45, won't always do it."

"Bone chuckled and nodded. "Asked him which hand he preferred...said, 'Don't matter none, which ever is closter'...Last I heard, he's had to kill eleven men in the line of duty."

"Really?"

"Yep...Course I like my .50 cal." He pulled out his Smith & Wesson 500 and held it up so she could see.

"Oh, my sweet Lord...That's like a hand cannon."

"Most powerful handgun in the world...Doesn't matter much where you hit them...they're going down...'specially when you use hollow points...But, I still like a head shot. It's kind of like dropping a watermelon from the top of the barn."

"I would imagine." Silke giggled and looked down at her little brother. "Time for you to hit the hay, young man."

"Aw, do I have to? Cain't I stay up an' listen to ya'll?"

"No, honey, it's been a rough day and tomorrow we have to take you to your Aunt Janie and Uncle Guss'. We're going to be chasing the bad guys that killed momma and daddy ." A look of pain crossed her face.

"Aw, Sissy."

"No more talk, come on."

Silke got to her feet, helped Billy up, and they walked holding hands over next to the tree trunk where she had made him a bed. Padrino gave her one of the extra blankets from the panniers for him.

"Unusual woman," said Padrino as Silke and Billy walked out of the firelight.

"Reminds me of Fiona," commented Loraine.

"Two peas in a pod," added Bone. "Notice? Same kind of eyes...Not the same color, but can look a hole right through you."

"I like her. Wonder if she'll be able to read Lucy?" asked Padrino.

"I expect we'll be finding out, eventually," said Loraine as she got up to brew another pot of coffee.

"I just can't help but wonder how Lenny got here," commented Padrino.

"Had to be an accident...like Loraine and me," replied Bone.

"Don't suppose he got hold of one of those *moldivite* impact crystals like you do?" Loraine asked Padrino.

"Could, but he would have to know how to use it with Zen meditation and find an electromagnetic vortex source point like the cave...Too many ifs and variables," the veteran Marine replied.

"I vote for accident. Kid's smart, but like Lucy said...the greatest minds on two worlds haven't figured out how this time travel thing works, yet," said Bone.

§§§

CHAPTER SEVEN

WALNUT BAYOU

"Where we headin', Big John?" asked Whitey as he cinched up his horse.

Tackett stabbed his foot in the stirrup and swung easily into the saddle. "Rubottom...'bout ten miles up the bayou. Needin' supplies, money, an' see as we kin pickup Taylor a wheelgun. They got a brand new mercantile there."

The others, including Lenny Taylor, mounted up and followed Comanche Bob, north alongside Walnut Bayou.

The early morning sun was shooting red and gold arrows across a partly cloudy sky giving harbingers of a crisp, cool January day.

The half-breed led the gang into the two-foot deep, clear, limestone-bottomed creek to hide their tracks. They would ride about a mile in the water and then exit at a good rocky bank on the east side.

Even though the creek was shallow, Taylor couldn't help but feel a twinge of fear of riding in the water. His abnormal apprehension stemmed from a near drowning episode with his brother when he was ten.

His older brother had drowned in the act of saving Lenny, creating indelible scars on his psyche.

He slipped his hand in his pocket and habitually rubbed the ancient Amerindian blue quartz crystal with the raised enigma symbol carved on it he found outside Aurora, Texas, in 2017, when he was hiking. He was also rubbing it during an intense electrical storm in 2018 when he was suddenly transported to 1899.

Comanche Bob led the gang a little to the east side of the main channel. The water was clear enough to see the bottom and the carp, cat, bass, bream, and minnows scattered in front of the hooves of the horses as they splashed along.

Almost a mile and a half north in the creek, Bob spied a rocky shelf tilting down into the water from the east side surrounded by dogwood, whoa vines and cedars. He nodded at the men behind him, reined his mount to the right and walked out of the water up on the limestone slab.

The water dripping from the horses onto the rock would dry rapidly even in the cool weather leaving almost no trace of their exit. They threaded their way through the brush and continued their trek north.

JUSTICE RANCH

The sun had cleared the tree tops as Silke rode back into the area in front of the barn next to the campsite. She dismounted, loosened *Issoba Lakná's* girth, watered him and then tied him to the corral next to the other horses, already tacked.

Silke walked over to the camp where Bone and Loraine were covering up the fire with dirt.

"Got some coffee left," said Loraine.

"Love some…That was so hard, leaving Billy with Mama's sister and her husband." Loraine handed her a cup. "Got to cry all over again. Aunt Janie and Uncle Guss said they'd tend to the animals and go into town and let the sheriff's office in Gainesville know what happened and that we're on the trail of the gang…They didn't know about Sheriff Durbin bein' shot," commented Silke as she took a sip of the tepid brew.

She pitched the balance and the grounds on the dirt pile over the remains of the fire, walked over and got her bedroll. "Ya'll ready?" she asked.

"Waiting on us, you're backin' up," replied Bone.

"Do what?" she replied.

Loraine chuckled. "It's a thing from our time, Silke…Means we're ready."

"Coulda just said so," she said.

"Thought I did," muttered Bone as he, Padrino and Loraine headed toward the horses.

Silke grinned and stepped up behind them.

"What's your horse's name?" asked Loraine as she mounted Sweet Face.

"*Issoba Lakná*...Chickasaw for Yellow Horse. He was given to me by a Chickasaw Lighthorse, *Nashoba Hommá*, means Red Wolf, I worked with him for over a year tracking down some rustlers. He taught me a lot about tracking...*Lakná's* my best friend."

"Always good to have a horse that you trust...and that trusts you," said Padrino.

"He's pulled my fat out of the fire more'n once...Knows what I'm thinkin', before I do sometimes."

"Horses like that are hard to come by," added Bone as he reined Hildebrandt to the left and led the group off to the north. "My guess is they're headin' straight for Sivells Bend."

"I'd say you were pretty close to being right, Bone," agreed Silke.

"Close only counts in horseshoes and hand grenades."

Silke's laugh was almost musical. "Never heard that before...I know, it's from your time."

"Wait until we talk to Stella and Peach on these." Loraine held up her Galaxy smart phone.

"What's that?"

"We call them smart phones," said Padrino.

"Phones? You mean like that communicating device, the telephone, Graham Bell invented?"

"Exactly," replied Bone.

"But, there's no wire," she said.

"It's wireless," answered Loraine.

"Oh, I read something in the Fort Worth paper about wireless telegraphy system that an Italian inventor by the name of Marconi came up with...you mean like that?"

"That was the progenitor of our phone system, but Marconi actually stole it from Nikola Tesla's patents, except we can send images through these in our time."

"You mean they work here?" Silke asked.

"Sometimes...Depends on if the girls we mentioned are near a particular energy source we have there that can work through the vortex I mentioned last night," answered Padrino.

"Oh, I got a headache trying to follow you."

"Don't feel bad, Silke, I get one too, sometimes, trying to figure it out. I finally just said, what the hell…it works. Not gonna look a gift horse in the mouth," said Bone.

"Now, *that* I understand…Who are that Stella and Peach you mentioned?"

"Stella Johnson is an Inspector with the Gainesville Police Department and Peach Presley is a forensics technician with the department. They're house and dog sitting our ranch in 2019," replied Bone.

"Sound like my kind of girls," commented Silke as she trotted up alongside Bone and studied the trail with him. "That the fella ya'll have been trackin'?" She pointed at the straight-sided hoof prints in the dirt.

"That's him," replied Bone.

"Mule footed on the back."

"Right." He looked over at her, impressed.

"Figured that had to be him. I already scoped out the prints of the gang before ya'll rode up yesterday."

"You can tell the difference of all those tracks?" asked Loriane.

"Oh, sure…One of 'em has rotated toes, so he'll break over quicker, another's just been shod, an' the nail heads are still sticking up a mite. That one there…" She pointed. "…has a bar shoe for a wall crack, left front, an' the smaller one over there, the right front is loose…gonna throw it sooner than later if they don't get it fixed. And see, there's one that's gettin' a little lame an' not pickin' his left rear up high as the right…settin' it down short. Probably got a pebble wedged in the frog groove."

"Dang, girl, you sound like Bass," said Bone.

She smiled. "Worked with Red Wolf for over a year, like I said. He was amazing…could tell a mare from a geldin', from a stallion, just by lookin' at their tracks…I can't get anywhere near that. But he taught me how to track through water and over rock."

"Wow, way cool. Think I'll let you take the lead then. Never had to do much tracking up in our time. I'm still on the learning curve…If it's pretty obvious, I can follow it."

"You done it long as I have, it gets to be second nature…Like watchin' my grandma cook. Used to ask for her recipe an' she'd just say, 'Oh, honeygirl, don't have any idea. Just mix till it looks and smells right…You'll get that way, too…when you've done it enough'."

They rode up to the wide sandy banks of the Red River at Sivells Bend. The breaks had gotten much thicker than during the cattle drive days since there were no cattle continuously tramping it down.

"I'd say lets just follow their tracks straight across. They apparently didn't hit any quicksand. Behind me, ya'll," said Silke as she nudged *Lakná* into the muddy water and out into the current.

Bone followed, with Loraine behind him and Padrino, leading Bart, following her.

They crossed without incident and clambered up the north bank to the right of a thick willow grove.

"Looks like they headed over to Walnut Bayou. It's a clear, spring-fed creek. Good place to camp...Good graze and water," said Silke.

RUBOTTOM, IT
CHICKASAW NATION

The Tackett gang had split up, with Big John and four others, including Lenny, entering from the south and Duce Walton and the other three, circling around and coming in from the north.

Big John's bunch reined up in front of Osborn's Mercantile. All, but the lookout and horse holder, Turkey Jim, dismounted.

Walton's group stopped at the small bank across the street from the mercantile. Everyone but Comanche Bob went inside.

Less than a minute later, shots rang out from inside both locations. Citizens on the street started running for cover, women screamed, and horses tied at hitching rails and hooked to buckboards panicked.

More shots were fired.

Inside Osborn's, Big John, shot two customers, a man and a woman, dead where they stood. He turned his pistol on the clerk behind the counter who was filling a tow sack with can goods and bacon slabs.

Tackett smashed the counter glass and removed a brand new 1875 Single Action Army Remington .44-40 and two boxes of shells, then he grabbed all the money from the open drawer of the brass cash register and shoved it in his coat pocket.

The clerk fearfully handed Lenny the sack, and then Big John coolly shot him between the eyes.

"Let's go," he said to the others as they were putting anything they fancied in the store in small flour sacks.

All four of the customers that had been in the store and the clerk, lay on the floor, dead or dying as the outlaws rushed out the double front door and mounted their horses.

Across the street, Walton and Salt Creek fired two more shots back inside as they exited the front door of the bank, grabbed their horses from Comanche Bob, mounted and spurred north down the street, joining Big John's group, firing their pistols at store fronts as they galloped out of town.

Noxious clouds of light gray gunsmoke drifted out of the open doors of the mercantile and the bank to blend with the fresher clouds outside, marking the devastation just visited on the small agrarian community in the Chickasaw Nation.

§§§

CHAPTER EIGHT

WALNUT BAYOU

"They camped here last night...left early this morning," said Silke as she felt the ashes of the camp fire.

She got to her feet, took the reins from Bone and swung up into her saddle. "Headed north."

They trotted out of the camp at an amble, north along the creek from the horseshoe bend Tackett's bunch had spent the night in.

"Entered the creek here," said Silke as she legged *Lakná* into the water and studied the bottom for a moment, then turned in her saddle. "Went north in the creek, thinkin' they could hide their tracks."

"How can you tell?" asked Bone.

"Come down in here an' I'll show you."

Bone bumped Hildebrandt forward down the bank into the creek. "Okay, what am I looking at?"

"See how that slime on the rocks is disturbed? They stayed in a single file...there, that line across the rocks on the bottom headed upstream is scraped off."

"Well, I'll be darned...Good to know," said Bone.

Silke reined her gelding up out of the water and trotted off to the north.

"Where're you going? Aren't you going to follow the tracks?" asked Loraine.

"No need...know where they're goin'," replied Silke.

"How?" asked Padrino.

"Nothin' to the west but Oklahoma Territory...it's pretty sparse. Right now, they have no idea they're bein' tailed. They're goin' to the first town this way, probably for supplies and money."

"That would be?" asked Bone.

"Rubottom," she replied. "'Bout ten miles."

They followed after her at a road trot.

Bone chuckled. "Just like Bass...Don't track 'em if you can go where they're goin'."

A little over an hour later they trotted into the little hamlet of Rubottom.

"Oh, damn, too late," said Bone as they observed the cleanup activity and the boarding over of windows at many of the stores.

"That would be a sheriff's deputy there in front of the bank," commented Silke.

She reined in the man's direction.

"Deputy, I'm Silke Justice...Pinkerton, this is Deputy Sheriffs Bone, Loraine Bone and Padrino...I have to assume the Tackett outfit hit your town?"

The fifty something lawman looked up at Silke, and then the others. "Don't know what the name of the gang was, but they hit us an' hit us hard. Kilt eight townsfolk an' wounded three more...Not a soul was armed, not one...Nine of 'em they was...Bloodthirsty a bunch I've never seen."

"Head north, did they?" Silke asked.

"Yep, hollerin' an' shootin'...Was like the Red Legs after the war...Took what they wanted, shot up the town an' rode off...purty as you please."

"Like to stay and help, but we better get on the trail after them," said Bone.

"If you catch 'em...they deserve a killin'...nothin' else," said the deputy.

"We know...When we catch 'em, no *if* about it," answered Silke with a trace of steel in her voice as she reined her gelding to the left and trotted on to the north followed by Bone, Loraine and Padrino.

She pulled *Lakná* to a halt about a mile out of town. They were still paralleling Walnut Bayou off to the west.

"Believe they're heading toward the Arbuckles, 'bout another forty miles. Need to rest our horses, they're not runnin'…Notice how they cut to a slow trot after they got out of town?"

"You say so," said Bone.

"Well, they did…Just look at the distance between their hoof prints. I suggest we go ahead an' make camp over by the creek an' give our mounts a good rubdown, some grain an' let 'em graze…We can make up time tomorrow. No sense in wind breakin' 'em."

"We'll follow you," said Loraine.

Silke nudged *Lakná* over toward Walnut Bayou. "Looks like a good spot there in that nook where the creek cuts to the west then meanders back north."

"Works for me," commented Bone as he and the others followed.

Padrino leaned over toward Bone. "Take charge type."

Bone grinned. "You think?"

Night had settled as they finished their supper of beans, bacon and hot water cornbread and were having coffee.

"How far behind do you think we are, Silke?" asked Loraine.

"Nine…ten miles, give or take." She took a sip of the hot trail brew.

"If we were a little closer, I'd do a little nighttime recon on them."

"How do you mean?" asked Silke.

"What I did in the Marine Corps in Afghanistan."

"We're at war with Afghanistan in your time? Like the Barbary wars when Jefferson was president?"

"Well, not exactly, that was with the Muslim pirates along the Barbary coast. They were capturing American ships and demanding tribute. Jefferson sent the Navy and a squadron of Marines to Tripoli in what was know as Battle of Derne in 1805. Didn't last long…As we say in our time…Kicked ass and took names."

Silke giggled. "Read about it in school, but we're still fightin' them?"

"We've been fighting the Muslims since the eleventh century, you know…the Crusades." He shook his head. "All over religion."

"So you were over there before you became a cop?"

"I was. Did a lot of behind the lines, night time work...plus sniping."

Silke nonchalantly placed her cup on the ground. "We have company," she whispered.

The others repositioned themselves so they had quick access to their guns.

"Well, ain't this a fine howdydo?" came a voice from the darkness near the creek.

Their response was the sound of four hammers being thumbed to full cock simultaneously and all four guns pointing at a large shape at the edge of the firelight...

CADDO CREEK

"Here you go, Taylor." Big John pitched him the Remington .44-40 he had grabbed from the showcase counter in the mercantile. Next, he pitched a box of ammunition. "Know how to use it?"

Lenny grinned. "I expect so." He opened the gate and began feeding the brass cartridges into the cylinder leaving the last one open for the hammer to rest on. He had gotten a blanket-lined canvas jacket while in Osborn's and he dumped the rest of the box of bullets in a side pocket.

"You can give it a test tomorrow," said Tackett. "You might make a hand if you can get over bein' sceered of the water."

"Can't help it, almost drowned when I was ten," replied Lenny as he opened the flour sack he took inside and pulled out a pair of brown square-toed, calf-high boots and a blue bandana that he tied around his neck.

He had also found a dark brown, wide-brim, low crown, Stetson that fit and wore it out the door. In addition, he picked up a yellow oilskin slicker, blanket and ground tarp at Turkey Jim's suggestion for his bedroll.

"Well, that's a bit better. Now you won't stick out like a sore thumb," said Duce.

"Where we headin', Boss?" asked Whitey as he cut a chaw from his plug of Brown's Mule Chewing Tobacco with his Green River knife.

"Well, on the off chanct that we are bein' tailed…we're gonna split up…Duce, you take yer bunch and head toward Davis, me an' my group will go to Hennepin." Tackett took a sip of his coffee. "We'll meet up to Wynnewood in three days, an' go to Oklahoma City from there...Easy enough to git lost in a big town."

WALNUT BAYOU

The large figure stepped forward into the circle of firelight, a big toothy grin spread across his face.

"Bass!" exclaimed Bone.

Loraine holstered her Kimber, got to her feet, walked over and hugged the big lawman.

"Got 'ny coffee left?" he asked.

She stepped back and looked up at him. "I expect so...Got some hot water cornbread patties too. I can fry you up some fat back, if you like."

"Be fine." He shook Bone's hand and looked over at Silke, and then Padrino.

"I mind you'd be Silke Justice an' don't believe I know this feller, but if I was a bettin' man, I'd say you'd be Padrino, Bone's godfather...Gotta be a story there on you bein' here."

Silke stepped forward with her hand out. "I am...But, how did you know?"

"Run into Red Wolf a while back...tol' me all about you. Said you wuz special, girl...real special."

Silke ducked her head and blushed.

Padrino stuck his hand out, too. "It wasn't me, I wasn't there, and I didn't do it."

Bass roared with his patented laugh. "Now I knows where Bone gits it...Pleasure meetin' you, sir." He pumped Padrino's hand.

"Where's Flash?" asked Loraine.

"He's over grazin' with yer stock."

"Wonder why they didn't let us know you came up?" questioned Bone.

"They knowed him an' me...old buddies, 'member?"

"Ah, right."

"'Sides, if'n I was a Shawnee, I'd be a sportin' all yer scalplocks on my lance...if I had one." He chuckled.

"We know. You're like a ghost at night...What are you doing in this neck of the woods?"

"Follerin' the same bunch you is, Bone...Tackett gang. Been tailin' 'em clean from Arkansas...They be a bad outfit...What'd they do that you're a trackin' 'em from Texas?"

"Murdered my momma and daddy down to Marysville...for no reason," replied Silke with a set to her jaw. "I'm gonna see that they pay."

"We were tracking a fellow that shot Walt Durbin after he robbed the bank in Gainesville and then he joined up with Tackett's bunch...He's from our time," said Bone.

Bass frowned and raised one eyebrow. "You don't say?...Walt dead?"

"Nope, Lucy managed to save him."

Bass grinned and shook his head. "Bless her...she's somethin' else."

Silke glanced at the legendary lawman. "You know about her, too?"

He nodded. "Could say so...Seen her do some wonderous thangs...Bone showed you what that bracelet she give him does?"

"Excuse me?" Silke replied and glanced over at the big man.

Bone grinned. "Not yet, Bass...Didn't want to scare her to death."

Silke cocked her head at Bone. "Nothin' would surprise me anymore."

§§§

CHAPTER NINE

CADDO CREEK

The winter sun had been slowly creeping up from the horizon for almost thirty minutes. The early morning dew sparkled on the brown, curly, buffalo, and blue grama bunch grass like millions of diamonds laying like a blanket across the bucolic rolling hills of this part of the Chickasaw Nation.

The fresh smell of the wet grass blended with the tantalizing aroma of the hickory-smoked bacon the gang had cooked for breakfast along with the strong dark Arbuckles coffee they had stolen in Rubottom.

Big John snugged up his cinch after tying his soogan on behind his cantle on top of his saddlebags. The others in his group, Bull Weatherly, Whitey Copeland, J.R. Duncan and Lenny Taylor were already mounted and waiting.

Duce Walton's group, Comanche Bob, Turkey Jim and Salt Creek Williams had already jog-trotted off to the northeast in the direction of Davis.

"Taylor, see as you can bounce a bullet off'n that big rock up yonder at the edge of the trail," said Tackett as he and Lenny trotted along the trail toward Hennepin ahead of the others.

"Can I stop?"

"Nope, might have to shoot sometime on the run. Just point, don't try to aim…Like pointin' yer finger, an' to be honest, kid, it's easier at a lope er gallop than at a trot."

"Never done this before." He heeled his grulla into a lope, thumbed the hammer back and fired. The .44-40 round ricocheted from the side of the boulder and whined mournfully off into the distance.

"Again," said Big John loping alongside.

Lenny reined his horse around and trotted back to where he started, turned and gigged his gelding into a lope again.

He cocked the Remington once more, pointed and squeezed the trigger. This time, the round hit more to the center of the rock, making a splatting sound.

"Better…You'll do," commented Tackett as he bumped his horse back to a walk.

Taylor followed suit.

WALNUT BAYOU

Bass finished burying the refuse from the overnight camp and covering the still live coals with dirt, but leaving the rocks around the pit for the next traveler.

He stopped, cocked his head and turned his right ear toward the Arbuckles in the distance to the north.

Padrino threw another half-hitch around the panniers on Bart to make him trail ready for the hills ahead.

Bone, Loraine and Silke finished tacking all the saddle mounts, including Bass' and Padrino's, and led them over to the campsite from the picket area.

Silke handed Bass the reins to his light dapple gray stallion, while Bone gave Padrino the reins to his claybank gelding, Star.

"Everybody's been grained, feet checked and groomed…Got rested and are good to go," said Bone.

"Much obliged," responded Bass. "Flash was a due a good brushin'. We been on the trail fer a spell…All the way from Texarkana."

"Well, let's head 'em up an' move 'em out, as the sayin' goes," commented Bone.

"Lead on, Silke," said Padrino.

"Oh, no, I'll defer to the master. Red Wolf told me about Bass' trackin' skills. I'm here to learn." Silke had a big grin across her attractive face. There was a field of freckles sprinkled across her small, straight nose.

"Can't argue with that," added Bone.

"Awrighty then, they be fair easy to track…Don't know 'nybody's back here. Purty hard to cover the tracks of eight er nine cayuses, anyhoo." Bass squeezed his big stallion into an easy trot over to the path.

He turned to Silke as they reached the main trail and headed north. "Heered a couple shots off in the distance jest 'fore we left…Had to have been eight, nine miles toward the mountains."

"Think it was them?" Silke asked the first black man to be appointed as a Deputy US Marshal west of the Mississippi.

"I mind," he pursed his lips under his thick, dark mustache and replied as Flash settled into a smooth single-foot.

Less than an hour later, they trotted into Tackett's former camp. Unlike Bone's cleanup and burial of the rubbish, the outlaw's camp showed evidence that no one cared about the litter—empty cans, butcher paper, a whiskey bottle, multiple cigarette butts, and the smell of urine permeated the air where they dismounted.

Bass and Silke checked the fire pit. The coals still smoked slightly.

"Left 'tween one an' two hours ago." Bass walked to the edge of camp, knelt down for a moment and then walked over to the east side of the clearing.

"Whatcha got, Bass?" asked Silke.

"Feared of this...They done split up."

Bone walked over to join him and Silke as they studied the tracks.

"Walt's shooter went with this bunch to the north," said Bone, as he pointed at the tracks.

"Uh-huh...Five went thisaway..." Silke pointed the same direction. "...an' four that way." She nodded to the northeast.

"They finally playin' it smart. Don't know 'nybody's back 'hind 'em...but split up anyhoo," added Bass. "Bet a bear sign they'll jine back together on up the trail a ways."

"Padrino, why don't you go with Bass...and Silke, you come with us...We'll each have good trackers that way," said Bone.

"Ya'll get some of the supplies out of the panniers and put 'em in your saddlebags…I'll keep Bart…I'm with Bass, think they'll get back together in a bit," added Padrino.

Everyone loaded up, mounted and headed out their separate directions.

WOODFORD, CHICKASAW NATION

Big John's group walked their horses down the single dirt street of Woodford. There were only four buildings in the town. A combination general store and post office, a blacksmith shop, a school house and a Baptist church.

Many of the residences were small log cabins with the trees being hauled from the Arbuckles. The plank wood and two-by-fours for the store and post office had been trekked up by wagon from Gainesville.

The outlaws reined up in front of Smith's General Store. It had been purchased from the original settlers, the Bywater brothers, by Wood Smith, for which the town was now named. They dismounted and went inside.

A gangly young man, no more than nineteen, welcomed them, "Ya'll come in. What kin I do fer ya?"

Big John glanced at the counter. "Like some of that hogshead cheese there an' some crackers, you don't mind...fer all of us."

"Yessir, want me to wrap it up er you wanna eat it here?"

"Oh, wrap it up. Ain't stayin' long enough to eat it...take a couple pounds of that peppered venison jerky, too...Oh, an' hand me yer cash box under the counter, there."

"Huh?"

"You deef, boy? Said hand me yer cash box...Damn, ain't sayin' it ag'n." Tackett pulled his Colt, cocking the hammer ominously.

"Yessir," the clerk nervously replied and set a well-used cigar box up on the counter.

Big John nodded at Lenny who opened the box, removed what little cash there was and stuffed it in his pocket. He looked at the young man.

"You gonna wrap our goods er not?"

"Oh, yessir, sorry, sir."

The young man pulled off some brown wrapping paper, piled the hogshead cheese, crackers and jerky in the middle. He unrolled some twine from a spool, wrapped the bundle and set it back on the counter.

Big John nodded at Taylor again to pick it up, and then squeezed the trigger on his pistol. The roar was deafening inside the store as the bullet impacted the clerk in the middle of his chest.

The boy staggered back against the back counter, looked down in surprise at the red stain spreading from a dime-sized hole in his faded blue cotton shirt, then collapsed to the plank floor like a limp dishrag.

"Hate it when I have to repeat myself," said Tackett as he waved the cloud of caustic gunsmoke from his face, and then grabbed a handful of butterscotch candy sticks from a jar on the counter and stuffed them in his pocket.

Bull Weatherly looked at the boss with disdain as he and the others followed him out of the store.

Lenny's face had turned a pasty white as he glanced back at the young man, only a couple of years younger than he was, before he stepped out on the boardwalk.

An hour and a half after Big John and the other four left Woodford, Bone, Loraine and Silke rode into the town. The locals were still milling about in the street, in a state of confusion.

"This doesn't look good," said Bone as he pulled rein in front of Smith's General Store.

They dismounted and approached an elderly farmer standing on the boardwalk peering through one of the front windows of the store at several people inside.

"What happened, old timer?" asked Bone.

He turned and squinted at Bone and the girls. "Who you be?"

"Deputy Sheriff Bone…This is my wife, Deputy Sheriff Loraine Bone and that's Silke Justice, Pinkerton detective."

The old man nodded and spat an amber stream of tobacco juice off to the side where it splattered on the boardwalk.

"Some fellers kilt young Nat Rice, fetched him dead, they did…an' he weren't even armed. Jest shot him dead fer the puredee meanness of it."

"Did you see it happen?" asked Loraine.

He shook his head. "Didn't have to, but his sister, Mary Ann, did. She was hidin' back in the storeroom a peekin' through a knot hole…Mean, jest mean as sin, they wuz."

"Five of them?" asked Silke.

"Yep."

"See which one shot the young man?" inquired Bone.

"Mary Ann said she thought it wuz the leader. Big man he wuz." He looked Bone up and down. "Not big as you, 'course…Seen 'em ride outta town, I did."

They exchanged glances.

"We got some ridin' to do…Let's get at it, ya'll," said Silke.

§§§

CHAPTER TEN

WASHITA RIVER

Duce Walton's bunch, Comanche Bob, Turkey Jim, and Salt Creek Williams waded their horses out to nearly the center of the fifty-yard wide river, and then swam them across the main channel. Their mount's hooves touched the gravel bottom a good one hundred feet from the east shore and they churned forward, gradually climbing up out of the water.

Comanche Bob was first to clamber up on the shore on a wide sandy bank where the river had once flowed in its inexorable way south to the Red River and eventually to the Mississippi.

"Damn, I hate wet boots," said Turkey Jim.

"Shoulda took 'em off an' carried 'em like I done."

"Guess everbody cain't be as smart as you, Salt Creek," replied Jim.

"Yep, reckon when the big man passed out the brains, I musta been fair close to the front."

"Hell, yer daddy probably tol' you to do it when you wuz a little fart," commented Duce.

"Naw, couldn't afford no boots, er shoes fer that matter, till I was purtnear growed...then had to steal 'em."

"Easier to make moccasins, like the Comanche...Make less noise, too."

"Yeah, but, Bob, cain't wear no spurs with moccasins," said Salt Creek.

"Huh...Never see Injun that need 'em," replied Comanche Bob.

"He's got a point, there," said Turkey Jim.

"Shhh," cautioned Bob as he held up his hand. "Someone come." He nodded toward the trail through the trees that bordered the river.

The four brigands split into pairs on a previously agreed upon ambush formation. Salt Creek and Turkey Jim headed along the river bank to the south, Duce and Comanche Bob did the same to the north, effectively bracketing the travelers.

A drummer's wagon, loaded with house wares and staples was being pulled along the road to the north by two mules. Two men, dressed somewhat garishly, sat in the spring seat of the box wagon.

Pots, pans, and wash tubs hanging on the sides of the box, clanged and banged loudly as the wagon rolled down the rutted road.

"Well, been a purty good day, so far, Mervin, my boy," said the chubby, red-faced man in a green derby holding the ribbons.

"I'd say so, Clyde. Those new green swirled graniteware plates an' cup sets are doin' the ticket. Mind we'll run out fair quick…'specially throwin' in the matchin' coffee pot along with our special…"

Duce stepped out of the brush on the side of the road, his blue bandana was pulled up over his nose.

He held his .44 Russian Schofield in his right hand. "Stand and deliver!" he commanded.

"Whoa up there, boys," said Clyde as he pulled back on the reins. "What's all this then?"

"This is what's commonly called a holdup, fat boy. Now chunk down yer cash box."

"Sir, we're just poor travelin' drummers. Barely make enough to keep body an' soul together," replied Clyde.

Comanche Bob walked out in front of the mules from the opposite side of the road. He was also masked and had his Colt in his hand.

Mervin and Clyde both cut their eyes from side to side.

It was obvious that Clyde Maywether was giving more than passing thought to lashing the mules and making a run for it.

"Better do what the man says," came Turkey Jim's voice from behind the wagon.

Clyde whipped his head to his right, quickly glanced over his shoulder and around the front corner of the box at the highwayman to his rear.

"Don't even think about it, lard ass," said Salt Creek as he stepped out from the river side of the wagon, right next to Mervin's shoulder, he was holding a sawed-off double barreled, ten gauge shotgun.

Clyde leaned over to Mervin. "I'd say we were surrounded by tobymen, lad. We'll have to buy our way out."

"You got three seconds to throw down that cash box," said Duce, as he cocked his pistol. "One…"

"We shall be happy to comply, sir. Dreadfully sorry for the delay…you caught us unawares, as it were," commented Clyde as he leaned backward and picked up a tin box behind him and handed it to Mervin. "Give this to that gentleman, my boy."

Mervin shakily held out the gray metal box to Salt Creek, who took it and carried it forward to Duce.

Walton opened the box, counted the bills and then the coins. "This all, fat boy?"

"It is sir. As I said we're just live-a-day drummers, selling house goods and hymnals to the rural citizens of the Chickasaw Nation."

"Climb down," said Duce.

"Sir, I assure…"

"Dammit, I said climb down or I'm gonna pull your fat ass out of that seat myself."

"As you wish, sir." Clyde wrapped the long reins around the brake lever on his right and stepped down to the road.

Mervin climbed down on his side.

"Now walk around here in front of these mules."

"Yes, sir," replied Clyde.

"Doff them duds," said Duce.

"I beg your pardon, sir?"

Walton just stared at the man and slowly raised his pistol to eye level and cocked the hammer.

"Right a way, sir," said a sweating Clyde as he began removing his clothing as rapidly as he could.

In a short couple of minutes, both men stood in the middle of the road in front of the team in their longhandled underwear—suits, vests, and hats were piled in front of them.

Duce nodded to Comanche Bob who walked over and started going through the drummer's clothing. He pulled out a long leather wallet from Clyde's coat and pitched it to Walton. Bob pocketed a gold watch and fob chain from Clyde's vest.

"Well, looky here, looky here." Duce held up a thick sheaf of paper money from the wallet. "You lied to me, fat boy."

"With God as my witness, sir, I merely forgot that was in there."

Walton looked at the wad again. "Uh, three hundred dollars?...I don't think so." He squeezed the trigger on his already cocked weapon.

Blood misted up in a cloud from Clyde's forehead as a hole appeared just above the center of his eyebrows, and he collapsed backward into the mules and then to the ground like a rag doll.

The mules snorted, brayed in terror and tried to back up as Comanche Bob quickly grabbed the lead mule's harness.

"I hate liars." Duce swung his pistol to Mervin. "You gonna lie to me, too?"

"No, sir...there's fifty dollars in my coat and a gold eagle in my vest pocket. You're welcome to them."

Walton glanced at Salt Creek and Comanche Bob. "Well, now, that's really nice of you, sonny...Idn't that nice, boys?"

"I never heard anythin' so nice, Duce," said Turkey Jim.

The front of Mervin's union suit suddenly had a growing wet stain that continued down his left leg and puddled around his brown brogans in the dirt.

"Think he needed to see a man about a dog, Duce," said Salt Creek. "But, there ain't no dog."

"That's nasty, boy...damn." Duce cocked and fired his Russian again, this time in the middle of Mervin's chest.

The young man cried out, grabbed his chest and dropped to his knees. "You have killed me." He fell over on his face in the road.

"Cut them mules loose an' go through the wagon. Bet a dollar they's some who-hit-John in there."

Turkey Jim was already up on the wagon and going through the back. In a short moment, he stuck his head back out the front drapes holding two unlabeled whiskey bottles, one in each hand. "Haw, Duce, these fellers was really whiskey peddlers. They's two cases of forty-rod in here."

"Huh, they's breakin' the law...peddlin' cheap rot gut whisky to the Redhides...We done our civic duty today, takin' care of hooch runners...Git what we kin use an' burn the rest, wagon an' all."

Bass and Padrino were within a mile of the Washita River when they heard a shot from the other side.

"Handgun?" suggested Padrino.

"Uh-huh…most likely a .44 or .45, I'm thinkin'."

They bumped their horses up into a lope in the direction of the river when a second shot sounded.

"They robbin' somebody er a stagecoach on the road what runs alongside the Gulf an' Colorado Railroad."

"They have a stagecoach going the same direction as a train?" questioned Padrino.

"Just for short runs from the stations out to the towns…mail, freight an' sech."

They reined up at the river bank and eased their horses down into the murky water.

"We'll have to swim 'em fer 'bout twenty yard out there just past the middle to cross the channel. Rest ain't too bad…'bout belly deep," said Bass.

They both slipped out of the saddle when they hit the channel and held on to their saddlehorns making it easier for the horses to swim. The pack horse swam along behind.

Each pulled themselves back in the seat when Flash and Star gained purchase on the bottom, forging their way to the opposite bank.

"See smoke, Bass…Above the trees," said Padrino as he glanced up river.

The big marshal looked at the white smoke curling above the tree line. "'Bout a half mile up the road…Mind they burnin' a wagon, most likely…Thinkin' we be suckin' hind tit…Hour late an' a dollar short."

§§§

CHAPTER ELEVEN

ARBUCKLE FOOTHILLS

Big John's bunch walked their horses along the wagon road as they climbed up the front side of the first outlying ridge of the mountains. The 1.4 billion year old granite thrusts poked up through the prairie grass looking similar to dragon's teeth as they were lined up in rows like they'd been planted by some giant farmer.

The ancient folded and faulted Arbuckle range was the oldest mountain range between the Rockies and the Appalachian Mountains. They were eroded down to only 1400 feet above sea level and were honeycombed with freshwater springs and miles of caves and caverns formed by underground water over the eons.

Tackett reached in his pocket and pulled out two pieces of the stick candy he had grabbed at the mercantile. "Want a butterscotch, boy?"

"Yessir, thank you," Lenny replied as he took the sweet confection and stuck the end in his mouth. "Wow, these are good…Don't have 'em like this where…uh…I'm from."

"That so? Where are you from, Taylor?"

"Uh, my folks, uh…live up in Kansas…Liberal, Kansas. But I'd been in Gainesville for the last two years, uh…workin' for the city."

"Doin' what?"

He pulled the candy from his mouth. "Oh, uh…bookkeepin'. I was a clerk."

"Huh…don't say? Must be purty smart…Ain't worth a damn at cypherin', myself."

"Kinda comes easy to me."

"Who was this feller you kilt?" asked Big John as they topped the first hogback.

"Uh…friend, or I should say…former friend."

"Oh, yeah, the feller you said betrayed you an' you planted a knife in his ribs."

"Yeah…He was hittin' on this girl…"

"Smackin' her around?"

"Uh…No…Flirtin' with her."

"Ah, treadin' on yer pasture, huh?"

Lenny glanced off at the wooded valley, with a spring-fed stream running through it on the way to its junction with Caddo Creek, below the ridge they were coming down. "Somethin' like that."

"Know what you mean…Don't tolerate that my ownself."

Tackett glanced over at a hollow down off to the west. There was smoke curling from a native stone chimney in a large four-room log cabin next to a big red barn. They were nestled in a nook beside a small branch flowing to the east.

Next to the house was the remains of a vegetable garden with only winter greens growing in one short row.

Several horses were eating prairie-grass hay along with a jersey milk cow in the paddock attached to the barn. The cow's calf was in a separate pen until the farmer could milk his mama.

"Well, I reckon we could use some home cookin'." He glanced over his shoulder at the others. "Meby the woman of the house did some bakin' today."

"Shore could use me a big slab of pie," said Whitey, with a giggle.

They reined down from the ridgeline to the homestead and stopped in front of the wide porch.

"Hello, the house," yelled Big John.

"What kin I do you fer?" came a voice from the front of the barn as a big, bearded man stepped out, still holding a three prong pitchfork.

He walked toward the house just as his wife, a Chickasaw woman, stepped out of the front door, wiping her hands on a dish towel.

Big John turned to the woman and doffed his hat. "How do, ma'am, we're passin' through an' haven't et today…Wondered if you had some victuals cooked up you might share with some weary travelers?"

She looked over the motley crew and finally said, "Hadn't started no lunch yet, but did bake up some carrot cake muffins." The Indian woman looked over to her husband as he walked up to the porch in front of the gang.

"'Spect as we kin spare a few fer ya'll…"

"Well, now, we wuz thinkin' of somethin' a little more substantial, say some smoked ham sandwiches…to go along with them muffins," replied Big John.

She glanced at her husband again. "No have any ham sliced up."

Tackett stared at her for a moment, and then squinted his eyes and said softly, but he might well have shouted, "Wadn't no request, squaw woman." He pulled his Colt from the holster and pointed it at her husband. "Git my meanin'?"

"Don't hurt us, mister." He turned to his wife. "I'll go out to the smoke house an' bring in a ham, Yellow Bird."

His wife nodded, the fear was palpable on her face.

"Now, that's the smart thing to do, pilgrim, you just do that," said Big John.

"Woman, you can go ahead an' bring out those muffins whilst yer waitin' on yer husband to bring in that ham.

She nodded an' turned to go back inside.

"Lenny, you go with her…she might need some help."

"I can do that," Taylor said as he dismounted and handed his reins to Bull. He climbed the steps and followed her inside.

"J.R., go with him to the smokehouse…See as you can grab a couple slabs of side meat, we're runnin' a mite low…didn't have none at that store.

"Awright, boss," Duncan said as he, too, stepped to the ground and followed the farmer around back to the small log smoke house.

Thirty minutes later, Big John and his men were mounting up. Several were still munching on muffins.

Lenny looped two flour sacks tied together over his saddlehorn. They were filled with the side meat, a ham, put-by peaches, and peas, with some fresh baked bread wrapped in a clean flour sack.

The farm couple stood side-by-side on the porch, the bearded man had his arm around Yellow Bird's shoulder.

"Well, folks, thankee kindly fer the grub. Mighty fine muffins they were, too, ma'ma." He tipped his hat. "Now, don't say nothin' 'bout us bein' by, ya'll...Hear?" said Tackett.

"No, sir, we won't. Don't know who you are, anyhoo," said the man.

"Let's keep it that way," said Big John as he drew his Colt and shot each in the center of the chest.

He holstered his shooter and looked down at the couple, still entwined in love, lying on the plank porch. "Dead folks cain't talk."

"Want me to fire the house?" asked Whitey.

"Naw, no need in sendin' smoke signals." Tackett looked up at the darkening sky. "'Peers as it's fixin' to rain...Hide our tracks. Would put out the fire, anyway...Bull, you an' J.R. throw leads on them two horses in the corral...Let's ride."

He wheeled his blood bay gelding about and trotted out of the farmstead back up toward the ridgeline. The others followed behind.

"That gunfire?" asked Loraine.

Both Bone and Silke nodded.

"Handgun," said Bone.

"Not good," commented Silke. "My gut tells me it's not some traveler shootin' at rattlesnakes."

"Agreed," added Bone just as the first drops of a winter rain began to fall. "Better get your slickers out, ladies." He glanced at the lowering clouds that seemed to stretch from horizon to horizon.

They dismounted, pulled their rain gear out of their soogans and slipped it on over their jackets.

"Looks like it's going to set in for a spell," said Silke as she too looked overhead.

"Joy," responded Loraine. "Glad I didn't have my hair done."

Silke glanced at her. "Do what?"

Loraine grinned, showing her even, white teeth. "Nothing...Back or up in our time, we have shops whose sole business is to wash, set, cut, style and sometimes color women's hair."

"You're pullin' my leg...What do you mean, 'color'?"

Loraine laughed. "Kid you not, Silke...Some, no, a lot of women change the color of their hair…on a regular basis. They lighten it, darken it, color it red, pink, green, put streaks in it…You name it," said Loraine.

Bone bumped Hildebrandt up into a lope toward the first of the upthrust granite ridges that marked the edge of the Arbuckle Mountains. Loraine and Silke followed suit.

"Pink? That's hard to believe…Why?" Silke asked as they loped along.

"Vanity. They think it makes them look better," answered Loraine. "Or just to draw attention."

"Amazin'…simply amazin'," commented Silke.

Loraine glanced over at the strawberry blond beauty. "Some need it, I would have to say…You don't, that's for sure."

Silke grinned. "Neither do you, my dear…neither do you."

"You should see me before I put on my makeup…Oh, wait, I forgot…I don't wear makeup any more." Loraine smiled.

"Somethin' else that's not necessary."

"Thank you. Guess we can form our own mutual admiration society."

Twenty minutes later they had covered the four miles to the homesteader's farm. The chilling rain was steadily beating a tattoo on their yellow slickers. There was still a spiral of smoke drifting up from the kitchen chimney as they rode into the open area around the house and barn.

Bone spied the bodies on the porch immediately as they dismounted and ground tied their horses.

He ran up the steps, knelt down beside the couple and felt for their pulses.

"They're dead," Bone said, shaking his head, as he turned back to Loraine and Silke.

"Your shooter's still with them," commented Silke as she glanced at the rapidly disappearing hoof prints out front in the rain. She looked up. "Headed north…Consistant."

Loraine glanced over at the barn some sixty feet from the house. "What's that?"

"What's what?" asked Bone.

"Heard something. Came from the barn."

Silke ran over to the red board and batt structure and flattened out against the outer wall next to the double-wide doors in the front. She drew her Colt.

Bone and Loraine did the same to the other side. On a signal from the big man, he and Silke whipped around simultaneously, at a crouch, inside and quickly stepped out of the backlight.

Loraine peered around from her support position with her Kimber .45 in the ready position.

Bone swept the area inside the barn with his .50 cal. "Clear."

They all heard a soft cry.

Silke moved over to the first stall and peeked over the top board. She holstered her Peacemaker, opened the stall door and went inside.

Loraine had come in the open door. She and Bone stood in the central alleyway, weapons still in their hands.

In a short moment, Silke stepped out of the stall carrying a black bundle next to her chest.

"Whatcha got there, Silke?" asked Loraine.

She looked, grinned and turned the fur ball over.

"Hey, that's a wolf-dog cross pup. Look at the size of those paws," exclaimed Bone.

The blue-eyed puppy raised his head and licked Silke across her mouth.

"Think you've found a friend," said Loraine with a big grin.

§§§

CHAPTER TWELVE

WASHITA RIVER

Bass and Padrino rode up to the smoldering drummer's wagon as the rain fell harder. They had donned their yellow slickers after crossing the river. Their collars were flipped up to keep the water from running down their backs on the inside.

Blackened pots and pans and shattered Mason jars were scattered in the burned remains of the wagon.

The mules were gone with their harness lying where it fell when they were cut away.

The sodden bodies lay in the middle of the road in front of the discarded harness. Blood stains on their union suits, from their wounds, had not yet washed away.

"Drummers...Robbed and murdered," said Bass. "Killed for no good reason." The venerable lawman's jaw muscles flexed in anger.

He glanced over at Padrino. "Won't be no quarter when we catches 'em."

"Are you going to give them the opportunity to give themselves up?" asked the retired Marine Master Gunnery Sergeant.

Bass nodded. "Ever bit of two seconds...Won't be no thinkin' 'bout it, ner cuttin' 'ny slack...They gonna git what they been dolin' out."

"'Do not be deceived: God cannot be mocked. Whatsoever a man soweth, that shall he also reap.'...*Galatians* 6:7," said Padrino.

"Yep, heered my ol' partner, Jack McGann, read that from the *Bible* mor'n onct." Bass glanced up at the heavy sky. "Reckon we best pitch our tarps till this rain blows over...Bury these pore souls when it stops."

"Looks like one of them's wallet's over there in front of the bodies," said Padrino as he dismounted, walked over and picked it up out of the mud.

"Mayhaps they's some papers in it what tells who the feller was...Mind the money's gone."

"You'd be correct on that, Bass."

Padrino fished through the long wallet, pulled out a folded Western Union flimsy and handed it toward Bass. "Somebody sent him a telegram."

"What's it say?...Cain't read."

"Oh, right." Padrino unfolded the thin yellow sheet. "To Clyde Maywether from Gilbreath Mercantile - Wynnewood, IT. 'In need of housewares and your special medicinal tonic on next trip...Stop...Percy Gilbreath.'...Must sell snake oil in addition to pots and pans."

Bass chuckled. "Not likely. I mind that's code fer whiskey. The houseware's is a good cover...Keeps the laws off'n they backs."

"Oh, that's right, alcohol's not allowed in the Nations, is it?"

"Nope, big chunk of my warrants is fer whiskey peddlin', an' bootleggin' in the Nations. They's saloons over in the Territ'ry west an' north of the Nations, though…Legal there."

ARBUCKLE MOUNTAINS

Big John led his minions toward a rocky shelf protruding out from the side of a block fault as the rain came down harder.

"Let's shelter under that overhang till the rain passes. Think they's even room fer the horses…Bull, see as what deadfall you kin find that ain't too wet for a fire."

"How's come you always pick me fer the blackbird details?" asked Weatherly.

Big John glared at the stocky man. "On account that's how I see you…Now, git it done."

Bull returned Tackett's stare for a moment, and then dismounted. Lenny took his horse's reins and the lead to one of the horses stolen from the homestead as his friend stalked off into the woods.

The ancient sedimentary layers on top of the granite batholith forming the cliff had been folded so many times they had taken on the semblance of Christmas ribbon candy. The softer layers of limestone and shale under the side of the granite intrusion sill had eroded away over the millennia to form a large hollow into the side of the cliff.

Whitey, you an' Duncan see as to settin' up camp an' gittin' a fire started…Could use some coffee…Taylor, you take care of the stock."

"What 'er you gonna be doin'?" asked Copeland as he stepped down from his saddle.

"Supervisin', albino…if'n it's 'ny of yer damn nevermind," replied an irritated Big John.

HOMESTEAD FARM

"What are you goin' to name him?" asked Loraine.

Silke looked down at the pup's clear blue eyes a moment, then up at the others. "Bear Dog…My grandfather had a big black part wolf mongrel he called Bear Dog. So, in honor of him…" She looked back down. "…call him Bear Dog."

"Considering the size of his feet, he may be big as a bear when he gets grown," said Loraine.

Bone reached over and scratched behind the pup's ears. "Tell you what do, Silke, hold his face up close to yours and gently blow into his nostrils a couple of times."

"What does that do?" asked Silke.

"He'll bond with your scent just like his mother. It works wonders. Bet you did the same with your horse."

Silke cocked her head and smiled. "I did...Red Wolf taught me that...Just didn't think about it for a dog."

"He'll know what you're thinking without you saying much. Ever watch a mother with her pups? Only occasionally will she have to orally communicate with them and then usually only to discipline them for their behavior."

"Very good, Bone...Very good."

She held the pup close to her, lifted his head with one hand and gently blew into his face over his nose three times. Bear Dog stretched up and licked her across the mouth again and snuggled his head under her chin.

"Bet you're hungry, aren't you, Bear Dog?"

He answered her with a short yip.

"Just as well camp inside the barn here…till after the rain. We can bury the farmer and his wife tomorrow in the same grave," said Bone.

"Here's a tarp you can wrap them in. Need to get them out of the rain…They're due at least that," commented Loraine.

"Babe, if you and Silke will strip the stock and give them a good wipe down with one of those tow sacks over yonder…looks like there's plenty of hay and stalls for them. Might even be some grain in here somewhere…I'll take care of the bodies," said Bone as he shook the dust and dead spiders out of the tan canvas tarp and rolled it up. "Build a fire just inside the doorway and start supper when I get back."

"Sounds good," said Silke.

He headed out into the medium-steady rain over to the ruins of the house. Bone glanced at the Jersey cow in the corral next to the barn. "Looks like Bessie out here needs milking."

"Bessie?" asked Loraine.

"The milk cow," he replied.

"I have no clue on how to milk a cow," said Loraine.

"Don't worry, Loraine, I've milked cows all my life," said Silke.

The Hispanic beauty glanced at her and grinned. "Not yet."

"Oh, right…Up to now, then." She glanced down at Bear Dog still in her arms. "Bet you'd like some fresh milk, wouldn't you?"

The pup squirmed in her arms and yipped again.

"Take that as a yes."

"Fresh milk sounds good to me, too," yelled Bone back as he continued on toward the charred remains to take care of his grisly duty.

Loraine and Silke led the five horses inside, tied them off and stripped their tack. They each took a tow sack from a pile at the opposite end of the alleyway, wiped the animals down thoroughly and combed their mane and tails out with a currycomb Silke had found.

"Aha," exclaimed Loraine as she lifted the lid to a wooden bin at the end of the stalls. "Oats."

There were just enough stalls for their three horses plus one for the cow and her heifer calf. They made sure the water buckets were full as were the feed bins in the corner. Silke forked over enough hay for each into their stalls.

"Here's a bucket you can use for milking. I'll wash it out over at the trough while you bring Bessie inside and put her in that end stall...You can put her calf in with her when you're done."

"Sounds good," said Silke as she finished filling the water buckets.

Bear Dog tagged after her every step, but was careful not to get directly underfoot.

He sat down beside her as she pulled up a three-legged stool. She leaned her forehead forward against the Jersey's tan flank after she had warmed her hands by putting them inside her shirt for a few moments.

Bessie glanced back at her, chewing on a mouthful of grain as Silke grabbed a teat from her strutted udder in each hand and rhythmically began squirting milk into the tin bucket on alternating strokes making a loud drumming sound as the stream hit the bottom.

Bear Dog made a slight whimper, raised one paw up in the air and looked up at her with his blue eyes.

"You can nearly talk, can't you?"

Silke angled one of the teats from the bucket in the direction of his face and squeezed. Without missing a drop, he caught the entire squirt in his mouth.

She grinned. "Well, think you've done this before, haven't you?"

The pup spun around twice, yipped, and sat back down for another squirt from the proffered teat—Silke didn't disappoint him.

Bone came back in the wide double-doorway after carrying the tarp-wrapped bodies and placing them under the lean-to at the side of the barn.

He gathered some soiled straw from the aisleway and then scrounged some dry scrap lumber from the back.

Bone made a small pile just inside the doorway and out of the rain that had slacked off to a heavy, but steady, drizzle. He had cleaned the old straw away from the fire site, to remove any hazard of the fire spreading.

Bone took the throwaway Bic lighter he always carried with him from his possibles pouch, and lit the straw under the small chunks of wood. The dried grass smoked for a moment and then a yellow flame curled up and devoured the hay, catching the wood on fire.

Silke brought in some stones she had found outside and placed them around one side of the small fire for the cooking utensils to sit on.

"Good fire placement, Bone. The breeze is from the opposite end of the barn. Carrying the smoke outside," she said.

Bone glanced back at the end of the barn and then at the smoke from the fire heading out the end they were at. "Huh...didn't even think about that when I was building it...Must be a gift...Well, rather be lucky than good, anytime," he said nonchalantly.

Loraine and Silky rolled their eyes. Bear Dog laid down next to his mistress and covered his eyes and muzzle with both paws.

§§§

CHAPTER THIRTEEN

DOUGHERTY, IT

Duce Walton, Comanche Bob, Turkey Jim, and Salt Creek Williams walked their tired mounts into the thriving community of Dougherty, formerly known as Strawberry Flats, as the light rain continued.

"Damnation!" said Duce as he looked around. "Place growed a mite since I last come through here…Two cotton gins, a asphalt plant, a newspaper, *The Arbuckle News*." He pointed. "Masonic Lodge…"

"An' a brand…spankin'…new bank," interrupted Turkey Jim. He pointed at a new two-story red brick building down the street on a corner.

"Bet they's a right smart of money in there, what with all these here new businesses…Not to say nothin' 'bout the railroad," added Salt Creek.

"Uhh, no want hit bank right now…Horses jaded. We no outrun posse. Must rest," said Comanche Bob.

"Don't nobody in this town know us from Adam's ox. I say we git a room at that hotel yonder, put the stock up down to the livery an' have 'em grained…We kin all take a bit of a rest an' somethin' 'sides trail food," replied Duce.

"Yeah, git some supper over there at Mae's Cafe, go back to the rooms an' have some of that tanglefoot we got from them peddlers, an' then come mornin' time…see 'bout makin' a withdrawal," said Turkey Jim, with a big grin across his face.

"Be nice to sleep in a soft bed, 'stead of the damn ol' wet ground," added Salt Creek.

ARBUCKLE MOUNTAINS

Deeper into the mountains to the west, near Lick Creek, Big John's group had set up camp under the porch-like gray granite sill that protruded from the side of the block thrust.

The area on and around the Arbuckles was heavily forested with pecan, hickory, sweet gum, cottonwood and post oak. Passageway through it was only by long established game trails.

"Weatherly, go find somethin' 'sides cedar fer that fire...Damn stuff pops and smokes too much."

Bull jumped up, did a mock salute and sanctimoniously replied," Yes, sir, Cap'n, right away, sir...Will there be anythin' else...sir?"

Big John glared at the stocky man. "Don't let yer alligator mouth overload yer jaybird ass, Weatherly."

Bull glanced over his shoulder with a half-grin at the leader as he walked back out in the soft rain into the woods and mumbled, "Aye, aye, sir."

143

"Smart-mouthed bastard's 'bout to push me too far," Big John muttered as he held out his cup to Lenny to refill."

Taylor took the cup from his hand with a glare of his own that was missed by Tackett's arrogance.

Lenny filled the tin cup to the lip and handed it back, sloshing some of the blistering, hot trail brew over Big John's hand.

"Damn you!" he yelled as he slung the cup and its contents to the side.

"Sorry, boss, guess I filled it too full," said Lenny as he picked the cup out of the dirt and carried it back to the pot to fill it once again.

"If I thought for one second you done that a purpose, I'd ventilate your hide right here." He stared daggers at the younger man as he carefully took the three-quarter filled cup with both hands.

"You kin start supper anytime, Whitey," he snapped at the albino.

"Yeah, sure thang, Big John. What's yer pleasure? We gots plenty."

"Heat up some of that canned corned beef an' sauerkraut with some fry bread, why don'tcha?"

"Whatever you say," Whitey said as he got to his feet.

HOMESTEAD FARM

Bone, Loraine and Silke lounged around the alleyway on loose hay, leaning against the plank stalls listening to the rain patter on the tin roof. Each had a blue-swirl graniteware cup of coffee in their hands.

"Looks like we could use some more wood and I think maybe it's time for Bear Dog to do his business," said Silke as she moved the pup's head from her leg and got to her feet. "Come on, son, you can go out behind the barn and I'll pick up some wood scraps on our way back."

She and Bear Dog headed down the alleyway to the other end of the barn.

Bone noticed her shapely hips in her tight riding pants with a leather seat insert as they walked away. "Dang! Girl's got an onion butt."

"What's an onion butt?" asked Loraine.

Bone took a sip of his coffee and then replied, nonchalantly, "Bring tears to a man's eyes."

Loraine backhanded the big man across his chest with a loud thump.

"Damn you, Bone, I'm goin' to kill you."

He held out his cup to keep it from spilling and giggled. "Just love gettin' your goat."

"You'll think 'gettin' my goat' when I lay another Kung Fu lesson on you like I did in Jacksboro, you big lug."

Bone sprayed half of his coffee out in front of him while the rest came out his nose. "Ow, that burns…Not sure I want to see that," he said.

"Well, keep it up big boy and you might see round two," replied Loraine.

"Round two of what?" asked Silke as she walked back up with an armload of wood pieces with Bear Dog prancing by her side.

She laid the wood close to the fire and put a couple of 2x4 pieces in the flames.

"Loraine turned me every way but loose before we got married, showing me some of her martial arts stuff." Bone looked over at the pup. "Is he smilin'?"

Silke glanced down. "I think so. He's done that every time I take him to go potty and when I squirted milk in his mouth…Don't know what you'd call him raising his upper lip like that, but a smile because he prances and wiggles at the same time."

"That's so cute," said Loraine.

"I'd venture to say that if he ever doesn't prance…that smile can easily become a snarl…Bad guys better watch out," said Bone.

"Think you were right about blowing in his nostrils, Bone. He already seems to know what I'm thinkin'," added Silke.

"I know." Bone cocked his head back and forth and smiled enigmatically.

Silke glanced at Loraine who just shook her head and grinned.

"What's that Kung Fu stuff you mentioned?" asked Silke.

"It's a Chinese form of self-defense with bare hands, and weapons like the staff…The art is known more specifically as *Wushu*. It involves strikes, throws, joint manipulation, and pressure point attacks…Much of it using the opponent's own weight and momentum against them."

"Maybe you'll have time to show me some of it."

"I can do that." Loraine grinned. "Ask Bone."

Silke nodded. "Sounds like it beats a killin'."

"Almost every time," replied Loraine glancing at Bone. "Tends to take the fire and belligerence out of drunks and bullies…quickly."

"It's a lot more fun watchin' it than being on the receiving end…trust me," said Bone. "Where do you think they went from here, Silke?" he asked.

"They've steady headed north from my folks place." She paused as she scratched Bear Dog's ears. "I'd say eventually…Oklahoma City, but anywhere along the way…I expect them to hit a place or two."

"That's the problem," said Loraine. "Knowing where they're going to hit between here and there."

"Wonder where Bass and Padrino are?" asked Silke.

Bone just pointed east.

WASHITA RIVER

Bass and Padrino had tied their ground tarps together and made a type of lean-to directed against the direction of the wind and the rain. Being in the woods helped keep a little of the weather off them.

The slow, steady rain dripped off the front of the tarps as Bass and Padrino sat underneath eating a cold supper of peppered jerky, hardtack and canned pickled peaches.

"This wouldn't be half bad if'n we hads some hot coffee to goes with it," said Bass.

"Maybe we can find some dry punk inside some bark of deadfall when the rain lets off," commented Padrino.

"You knows 'bout that, huh?"

"Part of our wilderness survival training in the Marine Corps."

"Thought them Marines was all on them big boats."

"Were, at one time, Bass, but as time went on, we started being the point of the spear, so to speak. First ones on shore, going behind enemy lines and sniping...Generally creatin' mayhem with the enemy and makin' it safer for those coming behind us."

"Kinda like Injuns, then?" said Bass.

"You could say that...If the Native Americans could have ever organized themselves and set up supply logistics, I think they would have driven the white man from these shores."

Ken Farmer

"Can't argue that none. Some of the toughest fighters I ever seen."

"The tribes spent hundreds of years fighting each other and they never could get along enough to organize. If they had, I'm afraid it would have changed things. When the whites slaughtered most of the buffalo, their main food source, that spelled the doom for the Amerindian…Such a pity."

"It is. They is a proud peoples…Love they culture. Lived amongst 'em fer two years when I run off from my massa durin' ya'll war."

"And we've pretty well destroyed it by cramming them into reservations and forcing them to be dependent on handouts from the government for their very subsistence."

"That's the way it is in yore time, I reckon?"

"Pretty much…And then they jump right in and fight the Japanese and Germans alongside us. The Navajo used their own language for the Marine Corps to communicate by radio in the Pacific theatre in World War II…The nips couldn't figure out what they were saying." Padrino chuckled. "But the Cherokee and the Choctaw started code talking for the US in World War I in Europe."

150

"They's lots of wars in yore time then?" asked Bass.

"You could say...War seems to be the natural state of man," commented Padrino.

Bass nodded and smiled resolutely. "Seems so, don't it?...They's always them what want somethin' somebody else has got...Whether they be outlaws er whole countries."

"I suppose it's been that way since Cain slew Abel," said Padrino.

"Reckon that's why they's folks like me an' you to sees they pays the piper...I mind Judge Parker's favorite expression was, 'It is not the severity of the punishment that is the deterrent...but the certainty of it'."

"Had not heard that, but I think it's dead on correct," said Padrino. "It's a problem we face even in our time...No certainty of punishment."

§§§

CHAPTER FOURTEEN

ARBUCKLE MOUNTAINS

The early morning fog following the overnight rain was thick enough to cut with a knife as Weatherly got up to stoke the banked coals to life and add wood. The trees at the edge of the camp clearing were barely visible through the murk and the silence, only dense fog can bring, blanketed the valley.

He grabbed the tin coffee pot and eased down the bank to the roiling creek that was now near overflowing from the eight hour rain and was churning its way down to Caddo Creek and then on to the Washita River. *Dang, fall in that an' I'll wind up down in the Mississippi and New Orleans*, he thought.

Bull filled the pot and worked his way back up the muddy slope to the campsite where he put a double handful of ground Arbuckle's Ariosa coffee in the pot. He set it on a flat rock close to the burning chunks of almost dry wood.

Lenny was the next in the camp to stir as he looked over at Bull first with one eye, then two. He sat up, rubbed his face with both hands, and then pulled his boots on.

"Coffee ready?" he asked.

"Not quite, Pard…few more minutes. Time you take care of your business, should be ready," replied Bull as he added a couple more sticks to the flames.

Big John, Whitey and J.R. still slumbered in their soogans on the chilly, dank morning, undisturbed by the conversation.

"Damn, kinda foggy this mornin'…an' still as death," said Lenny as he walked over into the woods at the edge of camp.

"It is," replied Bull.

The enticing aroma of the stout trail brew permeated the air when Lenny walked back into the area, buttoning the fly on his new canvas pants.

"Does anything smell better in the morning than fresh brewed coffee?" he added. "Especially when it's a damp and foggy one."

"Gotta agree with you there, kid," replied Bull as he wrapped one of his deerskin gloves around the handle of the pot, filled Lenny's cup and then his own.

Taylor reached out, took his cup and rolled it back and forth between his palms, savoring the warmth, before he took a sip.

He sat down on a log next to Weatherly to continue sipping on the warming liquid. "You and Big John don't seem to see eye to eye," he said softly.

Bull didn't reply for a moment, and then, "Been that way since I married his sister."

"Not good enough for her?"

"Could say that...Just waitin' fer it to come to a head." He blew across the top of his barefoot coffee, and then took a sip.

"Well, I got your back," Lenny whispered as he noticed Big John stirring across the fire under his blanket.

"'Blidged," replied Bull.

DOUGHERTY, IT

Duce, Comanche Bob, Turkey Jim, and Salt Creek Williams gathered on the front porch of the Arbuckle Hotel and peered across the street.

"Damnation, cain't even see the restaurant from here," said Salt Creek as he tried to look across the street through the morning fog at Mae's Cafe.

"Spooky," added Turkey Jim.

"Unnnh, bad omen. No like," commented Comanche Bob.

"Sound like a bunch of old women." Duce sneered at his men as he stepped down from the boardwalk to the muddy street. "Don't know 'bout ya'll, but, I'm ready fer some breakfast."

Duce disappeared into the heavy fog, followed by the others. They crossed the street and stepped up on the boardwalk just a little to the right of the door to Mae's.

"Sure glad we didn't have to look for it," said Salt Creek as he opened the tall half-glass front door, ringing a three inch brass bell attached to the header by a bowed piece of spring steel.

The four men entered the still mostly empty cafe and were overwhelmed by the tantalizing odors wafting from the kitchen—hot coffee, ham, bacon, sweet rolls and flapjacks.

"Umm, makes my mouth water jest standin' here," said Turkey Jim.

"You fellers take them hats off an' hang 'em on the rack there by the door. You don't wear your bonnet in my restaurant...Didn't ya'll mamas teach you anything?" asked a stout, heavyset woman with a coffee pot in one hand and a dish towel in the other that she slapped against her ample thigh for emphasis. "My name's Mae an' I don't allow rough language in here, neither."

"Yessum," said Duce as he jerked his worn slouch hat from his head. "You boys heard the woman."

The others followed Walton's lead and hung their hats on the line of wooden pegs on a board along the wall next to the door.

"Sit anywhere you like, I'll bring some cups...that's assumin' you want to start with coffee."

"Yessum, shore do," replied Salt Creek as he pulled out a chair and sat down at the nearest table.

"What 'er ya'll havin'? Got eggs, bacon, ham, sausage, biscuits an' gravy, grits and flapjacks. Make yer choice," she asked.

"Have hen eggs, blindfolded, bacon, biscuits an' gravy," said Duce.

"You'll eat the eggs like I fix 'em...an' like it...Next."

"Uh, reckon I'll take a big stack of them flapjacks an' a slice of ham. Like some buttermilk, too...you don't mind," said Turkey Jim.

Mae nodded and looked at Salt Creek.

"Biscuits an' gravy an' some of yer sausage, please ma'am."

"Unnh, me have flapjacks, too, an' bacon with grits." Comanche Bob bobbed his head once.

"Comin' right up," said Mae as she turned and headed toward the kitchen.

"What time you reckon the bank opens, Duce?" asked Turkey Jim.

"Most usually 'bout nine, I mind…We'll walk up just as they're unlockin' the doors."

"Might be purty quiet then, too," commented Salt Creek. "What with this fog an' all."

Duce nodded. "We'll go down to the livery an' git the horses tacked up an' tie 'em sorta spread out like 'long that side of the street where the bank is."

"What if they got one of them new fangled timer thangs on the safe?" asked Turkey Jim.

"Then we take what cash they got out an' haul ass. Cain't waste no time hangin' 'round waitin' fer it to open…'Course if'n it don't have one…" He patted the Remington on his right hip. "Might have to do some persuadin'."

"Might be easier if you was to have Comanche Bob here grab the boss man's hair an' put his knife against his forehead like he's agonna scalp 'im," suggested Salt Creek.

Walton cocked his head and turned to Williams. "Damn, Salt Creek, you're usin' yer head fer somethin' 'sides a hat rack, ain'tcha?…That's good. Put the fear of God in 'im an' don't make no noise."

"Lessen the banker gits the urge to scream bloody murder," added Turkey Jim.

Duce looked at the man and frowned.

HOMESTEADER FARM

Bone, Loraine and Silke finished snugging up their cinches in the alleyway. They had already turned the cow out into the pasture behind the barn with her calf.

"How're you going to carry Bear Dog, Silke?" asked Loraine.

"In my lap. I think he'll ride there just fine, between me an' the saddlehorn," she said as she slipped her rawhide bosal over his nose.

"You say so," said Bone. "He is too little to run along side and that's a fact."

Loraine glanced out the open front doors of the barn. "How are we going to know which way to go. That fog's thick enough to eat."

"In the Corps, we had to train on knowing what direction north was without a compass. Saw this study that showed that most people have an instinct on direction like migrating birds...Something to do with the Earth's magnetic field. You have to feel it."

"Bone, sweetheart, I love you to death...but sometimes you are so full of crap," quipped Loraine.

Silke giggled.

"Well, I also checked which way north was when we rode up yesterday...If there's a way to cheat, I'll find it."

"I know," replied Loraine.

"How long did you say ya'll had been married?" asked Silke.

"Only a couple of months, but we've been partners for over four years...Kinda like being engaged," replied Bone.

"Except for the number of times we threatened to kill one another...We couldn't stand each other until we figured out that we were actually in love," added Loraine with a big grin.

"Ooh, I *gotta* hear that story," said Silke. "Sounds juicy."

Bear Dog licked her face as she picked him up and stepped up into *Lakná's* saddle.

BONE'S ENIGMA

WASHITA RIVER

Bass and Padrino struck camp and saddled up before the ambient light from the rising sun brightened the sky high above the pea-soup fog that lay over the entirety of the Arbuckle area like a shroud.

"Where do you think they were headed?" asked Padrino.

"I mind they be goin' through Dougherty. It be right up the road what runs 'long the river...They been steady headed north since we left Texas...no reason to think they'll change now."

"That's what you were talking about a while back on not worrying about tracking...just go where they're going...How far is it?"

"'Bout five miles, I 'spect...If they's a mind to do any mischief, it'll be this mornin'."

Padrino mounted Star and dallied Bart off and nodded. "Let's ride, then."

Bass grinned and stepped easily into his light dapple gray Saddlebred stallion's saddle and they headed back over to the road, then north.

Forty minutes later, Bass pulled rein at the edge of town. "Let's lead the boys in an tie 'em up over to the mercantile…It's 'cross the street from the new bank they gots here."

"Sounds good, but we can't even see across the street."

"That gate swings both ways," Bass replied with a grin.

§§§

CHAPTER FIFTEEN

ARBUCKLE MOUNTAINS

Big John sat up, rubbed the sleep from his eyes and looked around the camp. "Damnation, fog rolled in durin' the night."

"Good observation there, Boss," sniped Bull.

Tackett's eyes shot steel daggers at the man squatted by the fire and ground his teeth. "Don't suppose you made coffee yet, Weatherly?"

"Just so happens I did."

"You gonna pour me a cup?"

"Oh, you want one? Shoulda just asked," replied Bull as he picked up the pot with his glove and filled a tin cup. "Reckon you want me to bring it to you, too?"

"Damn you…" snapped Tackett as he threw back his blanket.

Lenny took the cup from Bull and got to his feet. "I'll bring it." He stepped over to Big John and handed him the coffee. "Here, Boss."

Tackett got to his feet and took the cup from Lenny, still glaring at Bull.

"What time we headin' out, Big John?" asked Whitey.

Tackett looked out at the dense fog. "No rush. Gotta cross Wild Horse Creek an' I 'magine it's probably up some due to the rain. Should go down fair fast though…Head out after a little breakfast." He took a sip of his coffee.

HOMESTEAD FARM

Silke led out along the farm road to the north in the direction of the pass that cut though the Arbuckles where Wild Horse Creek was.

Bear Dog snuggled in her lap with his head up, peering to the left, and then to the right around *Laktna's* neck into the gloom of the fog-shrouded woods on both sides of the trail.

The thick mist coated everything with a layer of moisture. Bone, Loraine and Silke wore their slickers to keep their clothing dry until the fog lifted.

"Are those buckskins warm, Loraine?" asked Silke over her shoulder.

"Much warmer than cotton or even wool. Just don't want to get them too wet...takes longer to dry."

"May have to get me a set for trail work," she replied.

"That's why we did...at the suggestion of both Bass and Fiona. Matter of fact, it was Fiona's grandmother and some of her friends up in the Cherokee nation that made these for Bone and me to our measurements."

"My goodness, that's so wonderful...Love the bead work."

"Shouldn't be a problem to get you a set ordered after we introduce you to Fiona and Mason when we get done with this exercise," added Bone.

"They're actually doeskin...Softer than buckskin," said Loraine.

"Oh, right," Silke replied. "Good to know."

"It's amazing how quiet it is in the middle of a fog," commented Loraine.

"Even though it didn't happen very often, we always tried to move equipment in Afghanistan when it was foggy because sound doesn't carry well then."

"Noticed," replied Loraine.

"Course it's also good for zombies to roam around in," said Bone.

"Do what?...Zombies?...You mean dead people that rise up from the grave?" exclaimed Silke.

"Something like that," commented Loraine. "Might I remind you that Bone is somewhat of a practical joker...So, be prepared."

"Well, the Arbuckles *are* said to be haunted...'cordin' to the Chickasaw," said Silke.

"Yeah, Bass's partner, Marshal Jack McGann, told us about the ghost of his wife Angie's daughter, who drowned when she was swept over Turner Falls, her name was Anna...Said he saw her and she talked to him. She saved his life when he was shot and crawled up into that cave behind the falls."

"Really?" exclaimed Silke.

"What he said," replied Bone. "He had what *Anompoli Lawa*, the Chickasaw Shaman, called a spirit wolf...Snow white with gold eyes and huge...Name was 'Boy'. Now has an offspring he named 'Son'."

"Would love to meet Jack and Angie," said Silke.

"Probably going to happen...They live at Turner Falls on the east side of the Arbuckles," replied Bone. "Not too far from here."

Silke led the three along a zigzag trail up to the top of the first major ridge of the Arbuckles. The fog up there was thinner, but not that much. Visibility was still less than fifty feet.

"This is some kind of spooky fog," commented Loraine as they plodded along the muddy trail up to the top of the ridgeback.

"Any kind of tracks left, Silke?" asked Bone from behind her.

"An occasional gouge in the mud where one of their horses slipped a little," she replied.

"I suspect they went to ground well before the rain stopped," said Bone. "How far you reckon they got?"

"Hard to tell…My guess is somewhere between here an' Wild Horse Creek…Doubt they got that far," answered Silke.

"We could ride right up on them in this fog," commented Loraine.

"Got a point there, Pard," said Bone. "Probably be a good idea to pull up till this soup starts to clear…be about ten or so, my guess."

"Looks like there might be some clear space over there to the right. We could make some coffee and there's some yellow hop clover and vetch comin' up for the horses," suggested Silke.

"Works for me," replied Loraine as she reined Sweet Face over off the trail.

"I'll see if I can find some semidry wood over on the downhill side," Bone said as he pointed to the left where the woods started again.

He dismounted and handed Loraine the reins to his gelding, Hildebrandt, and quickly disappeared into the fog downhill.

Silke dismounted next to part of the granite thrust outcrop. She set Bear Dog on the ground and he instantly ran over to a large rock and hoisted his leg. He scratched the ground with all four feet and rolled over in the new green winter rye and clover.

After she loosened *Latkna's* cinch and hobbled him on the clover, Silke turned to the pup. "That feel good, Bear Dog?" asked Silke as she moved a few smaller rocks over to form a fire pit.

He spun around twice and yipped.

DOUGHERTY, IT

"Need a refill?" asked Mae as she walked up with her coffee pot.

Duce glanced up at the Regulator Ansonia clock on the near wall—it was five minutes before nine.

"Oh, think not, ma'am…We got things to do. Ain't that right, boys?"

The three men all grinned.

"Awright, then, it'll be two dollars for the four of ya," she said.

Duce dug into his vest pocket and pulled out two Morgan silver dollars and a quarter. He laid them on the table. "Mighty fine victuals, ma'am, mighty fine...The extra quarter is fer you."

Mae scooped the coins up and dropped them in her apron pocket. "Glad ya'll enjoyed it. You'll have to come back in for the noon dinner. Got fried chicken today."

"Well, sounds right tasty, ma'am, but we'll be leavin' town soon as we take care of our business."

"Too bad...You'll have to drop back in next time you're through this area."

Duce and the others got to their feet.

"We'll do that...Shore will," he said as they moved over to the wall to get their hats.

Bass and Padrino took their positions cattycorner from the bank. They could barely make out the two-story red brick bank building through the thick fog.

"I'm goin' to go over an' go in the bank like I's a customer when they's come in. You cover the outside case 'ny of 'em makes a run fer it."

"Still think they're going to hit the bank?"

"I does…Lots of new businesses here in Dougherty in the last year…It be thrivin'. That's the thing 'bout the marshalin' business…gots to think like the miscreants does."

"Where do you think they have their horses?"

"Mind they be meby two in front of the bank an' the others down next door at Mae's Cafe…They be one of 'em outside with the horses."

He nodded at Padrino and stepped off the boardwalk and headed toward the bank. He heard someone inside turn the lock just as he got to the door.

Bass turned the knob of the nine-foot tall, half-glass, right hand door and stepped inside, ringing the overhead bell.

"Good mornin', sir. Welcome to the Merchant and Planters Bank. How may we help you?" asked the slight-built, twenty-something teller.

"Oh, jest be needs to trade some paper money fer some silver dollars. I seem to keeps track of coins better'n foldin' money."

171

Ken Farmer

"Yessir, right this way." The young man adjusted his gray suit jacket, and then his burgundy cravat and stepped over behind the teller's counter.

He went to the barred window nearest the far wall. Bass followed him over and stood in front of the station.

Behind the three tellers, a portly gray-haired man with mutton-chop whiskers leaned over and spun the two dials on the four-foot wide, six-foot high Cary Company safe with Merchants and Planters Bank in gold leaf lettering on the door. He turned the chrome handle and pulled the heavy door open.

The three tellers stepped behind him to receive their cash drawers for their stations as the bell over the door tinkled again and a well-dressed woman stepped inside. She turned to the man in the somewhat rumpled dark three-piece suit who was holding the door for her.

"Thank you, kind sir," she said as she nodded to him.

"Yes, ma'am," said Salt Creek Williams as he touched the brim of his hat and followed her inside.

Comanche Bob and Turkey Jim opened the door next and stepped in the bank behind them.

Duce waited outside, mounted on his blood bay gelding fifteen feet from the two horses tied out front of the bank.

Walton took out his makings, built a quirly, got a match from his vest pocket and lit it with his thumbnail. He blew a cloud of smoke that instantly mixed with the fog over his head and then disappeared.

Comanche Bob stayed by the door to make sure no one else came in.

Turkey Jim approached the well-dressed heavyset man that had opened the safe. He drew his Colt.

"Awright, pilgrim, you jest turn around and get whatever cash and gold you got in that safe an' don't give me no sass."

Salt Creek drew his Remington, waved it around at Bass, then the woman, and finally at the second teller. He slid a ten pound flour sack under his barred window.

"All your cash...Now. Ain't gonna say it twice."

Bass grinned at the third teller who had stacked ten Morgan silver dollars on the counter in exchange for the ten dollar bill.

The big marshal started softly singing a Christian hymn written in the late 1700s, *"Amazing grace! How sweet the sound that sav'd a wretch like me!...I once was lost, but now am found...Was blind, but now I see. 'Twas grace that taught my heart to fear...And grace my fears reliev'd..."*

Turkey Jim turned. "Who the hell's doin' that sangin'? That you, Nigger?...Stop it!"

Bass chuckled. "I likes sangin'. Meby it'll help ya'll's souls when I sends you to God."

"What? Who the hell do you think you are?" said Jim as both he and Salt Creek cocked their pistols at the big black man.

"Oh, I don'ts have to thank on it much," He drawled slowly. "I already knows...On account that some folks calls me one thang an' some calls me 'nother..." He chuckled again. "But, mostly they calls me Bass Reeves...Deputy United States Marshal Bass Reeves..." He had a big grin across his face under his broad mustache. "...an' this jest ain't gonna be yore day, boys."

Salt Creek exclaimed loudly, "Bass Reeves?"

He and Jim both raised their pistols simultaneously. The ear piercing roar of gunfire echoed in the lobby of the bank along with billowing white clouds of gunsmoke.

The woman screamed and fainted…

§§§

CHAPTER SIXTEEN

ARBUCKLE MOUNTAINS

Big John and his gang had finished breakfast and broke camp. He led the single line of the four men on their horses down the mountain toward Wild Horse creek. The fog had only thinned slightly with the coming of the sun trying to penetrate the gray, leaden and depressing atmosphere. Visibility was less than fifteen feet.

The horses occasionally slipped in the muddy game trail zigzagging down the steep incline. The silence was eerie—no birds, insects, hunting hawks, or any other normal wildlife sounds—if there were any to begin with—could penetrate the caliginous mists.

The only sounds that could be heard was the snorting of the nervous horses and the creaking of saddle leather as they navigated their way down toward the creek in the valley below.

Lenny was as nervous as the horses, if not more so, not only by the shadowy fog, but also of the upcoming crossing of the rushing creek. He was third in line directly behind Bull, in front of J. R. and had one hand in his pocket, rubbing the silver dollar size ancient blue crystal with his thumb.

Thirty minutes later, they approached the turbid creek. Big John raised his hand for all to stop while he studied the fast moving water.

"Believe she's gone down 'bout two feet from the high watermark. Should be able to git 'cross awright without no problems."

"Should?" questioned Lenny.

"Ain't no guarantees in life on anythin', boy. Jest suck up yer belt an' foller me, Whitey an' Bull…We'll go first."

He looked downstream a ways. "We'll give 'er a try down yonder, this side of them rocks. Looks a mite deeper, but them rocks 'er slowin' her down some…Let's go."

He bumped his paint gelding, reined to the left about forty yards and eased into the water. "Bottom's good, gravel, no quicksand," he yelled over his shoulder as his horse moved on out to the middle of the swirling creek.

Whitey followed right behind him as Bull turned his mount to the side to speak to Lenny.

"Now, if the water gits deep enough fer your horse he has to start swimmin', slip outta the saddle an' hold on to the saddlehorn so's yer weight don't push him under…Hear me?"

Lenny was so scared all he could do was nod as Bull nudged his horse out into the water.

He glanced back over his shoulder. "Come on, boy. It won't take long. Horses is good swimmers."

"Does he know that?" Lenny croaked.

Out in the middle of the creek, the water had gotten deep enough the horses would have to swim for the opposite bank. Big John had already slipped from the saddle and held onto the saddlehorn as his paint swam another ten yards and finally was able to grab some purchase on the rocky bottom.

Whitey followed suit and held on to his saddle until his horse could touch bottom. He pulled himself on the saddle, swung his right leg over and picked up the reins as his toes found the stirrups.

Bull was doing the same and was almost far enough across that his horse could reach bottom when he heard Lenny scream behind him.

"Oh, God, oh, God," he yelled as he missed grabbing the saddlehorn.

"Grab his tail, boy!" Bull shouted, but to no avail—Lenny missed that, too.

His animal was panicked by the screaming and lunged toward the bank, sans his rider.

Taylor floundered in the current, going under, and then coming up, sputtering, flailing his arms, and screaming as the water carried him downstream toward more rocks.

Bull turned his horse in the shallow, knee-deep water near the bank, undid his rope and built a quick loop.

He twirled it twice over his head and cast it out in front of Lenny. "Grab the rope, boy, grab the rope!"

Lenny flailed his arms again, reached for the rope, still on the surface. He missed that, too.

"Help, help me!" he screamed.

Bull quickly coiled rope back in and built another loop as his horse splashed in the shallows along the bank. The hemp rope was now much heavier than it was because of the water and he was able to throw it further.

"Grab it," he yelled.

DOUGHERTY, IT

Comanche Bob, burst through the doors outside as the first shots rang out inside.

"Hold it," shouted Padrino as he charged from two doors down the street from the bank.

Bob turned and snapped two shots at the venerable retired Marine. Padrino never slowed as he rapid-fired his 1911A Colt with a two-handed grip as he advanced on the outlaw.

Comanche Bob fanned three more shots as all four of Padrino's shots drilled him center mass, not a half inch apart. The multiple impacts staggered the half-breed back along the boardwalk where he crumpled over toward the street. His limp form landed half in the muddy street and half on the boardwalk.

At the first sound of a shot from inside, Duce spun his horse around, spurring it viciously down the street.

Padrino turned and snapped three shots in his direction, but he had already vanished into the fog, leaving only the rapidly diminishing sound of pounding hooves in the murk.

Inside, Bass stood over Turkey Jim and Salt Creek's bodies with a .38-40 in each hand. The acrid gunsmoke was thicker than the fog outside.

The bank president peeked from behind the counter where he had ducked down when Turkey Jim first told Bass to stop singing. He slowly got to his feet.

"My God in Heaven, never in all my borned days seen anything like that. They had you dead to rights, Marshal." He wiped his sweating brow and pate with his handkerchief.

Bass nodded. "They thoughts so, too, but they eyes ain't near as fast as my hands. By they time they seen my guns comin' out of my holsters, it was done too late…Plus, they wuz panic shootin'…couldn't hit a bull in the butt with a broom…"

He turned to the woman being helped to her feet by one of the tellers and doffed his hat. "Pardon the language, ma'am."

The woman waved her lace hanky in front of her face. "With what you did today, Marshal, you may say what ever you please…You earned it."

"Jest doin' my job, ma'am, jest doin' my job. Onlest thang I wants is my ten silver dollars." He glanced at the first teller.

The door opened and Padrino stepped in and looked around. "About what I thought."

"How'd it go out there?" asked Bass.

"Got the door man, the guy watching the horses took off down the street like a scalded dog and disappeared into the fog. He's long gone." Padrino looked around again. "Looks like we won't find out who he was, now."

"Not likely," commented Bass. "Lessin' they's somebody heard his name if theys stayed at the hotel er got some breakfast over to Mae's."

Padrino glanced down at his canvas Carhartt jacket. "Son of a gun," he exclaimed.

"What is it?" asked Bass.

He examined both sides of the garment. "Got three holes in my jacket. Close...but, that only counts in horseshoes and hand grenades. "Fellow outside has four in his chest that can fit inside my hand." He held up his left hand. "We did a lot of Close Combat Drills in the Marine Corps, so it wasn't much of a problem in the field...Been there, done that."

Bass turned to the bank president. "Ya'll gots a Lighthorse er a town marshal?"

The banker nodded. "Town marshal. He's probably having breakfast about this time across the street at Mae's...He's usually not stirring around until around ten or so."

"Well, come on, Padrino, breakfast is on me."

"Let the bank catch your breakfast, Marshal...least we can do."

"Not necessary, sir, jest doin' my job."

"You for sure an' be danged, Marshal Bass Reeves?" asked the first teller.

Bass grinned. "Last time I checked, son."

"Good gosh almighty," he said as he handed Bass his stack of Morgans.

Bass and Padrino walked out the door and stepped over Comanche Bob's body laying sprawled at the edge of the boardwalk, his upper body was in the street.

"Hope the town's got an undertaker to clean this mess up," said Padrino.

"Most does…Got's to turn 'em in fer the re-wards, anyhoo. Knows that was Turkey Jim an' Salt Creek Williams inside an' that be Comanche Bob we jest stepped over. Needs to find out who it was what run off," said Bass as he opened the door to Mae's.

"Come right in. Welcome to Mae's…Well, I'll be…Hydee, Bass. That you doin' all that shootin' out there?"

"How do, Mae. Done part of it. Some malefactors wuz tryin' to do wrong an' make a illegal withdrawal at the bank."

"What's that you say?" asked a corpulent man sitting at a table with a large stack of half-eaten flapjacks in front of him and a white napkin tucked into his collarless once white shirt.

"He said there was an attempted robbery at the bank," said Mae.

"How's that?" the town marshal cupped his hand to his ear.

Mae turned to Bass. "He ain't heard it thunder in years." She leaned over and yelled. "Some men tried to rob the bank!"

"They're gonna swab what?"

"Rob the bank!" she yelled.

He shook his head making his jowls jiggle. "No, I was at the bank yesterd'y. Had to cash my check."

Mae rolled her eyes. "Never mind, just eat your breakfast."

"Think I'll eat my breakfast, you don't mind?" He stuffed a big forkful of pancakes dripping with syrup in his mouth.

Mae shook her head and led Bass and Padrino to a table. "What are ya'll havin' Marshal?"

"Some information first, Mae. Was there four fellers in fer breakfast this mornin'?...Strangers?"

"There was. Ate like it was goin' out of style."

"Git 'ny names?" asked Bass.

"Only one. Took him to be the leader. One of 'em called him, 'Duce'."

Bass nodded. "Duce Walton…Thought as much…Rides with Big John Tackett."

"Now, what ya'll havin'?"

"Have four eggs, any way you fix them, bacon with biscuits and sausage gravy…And milk, but, take some coffee now," said Padrino.

Mae smiled and bumped Bass's shoulder. "Like him…Easy to please."

"You wants to keep him?"

Padrino kicked Bass's shin under the table.

§§§

CHAPTER SEVENTEEN

ARBUCKLE MOUNTAINS

Silke led the way out of their camp along the top of
the ridgeline. The rising sun brightened the gloom
considerably, even though the fog was thinning, but
still present.

"Tracks are prominent," Silke said, looking back. "Don't think they realize they're being tailed."

"At least we can see almost thirty yards now," added Bone.

The trail led down the slope toward Wild Horse Creek in the distance. The topography flattened out off to the left of the trail against a vertical thrust outcrop with a large granite sill sticking out. There was a smaller creek to the right that drained back toward Caddo Creek—it was up, also.

"Made camp here in this alcove." Silke stepped off *Lakná*, set Bear Dog down so he could water a bush and she felt of the rocks around the pit. "Fire's been dead for about two hours…Been gone 'bout that long, I'd say. Waited till the sun was well up, probably about ten, before they broke camp."

Silke picked Bear Dog back up and swung easily into her saddle. "Smart for us to stop back there…Good idea, Loraine. We would have never seen this camp…or them earlier."

"My sweet Double D does have some good ideas on occasion."

Loraine's brown eyes snapped at the big man. "Bone…"

He grinned. "What?"

"You know what."

Silke chuckled. "I just love ya'll to death. You act just like my momma and daddy did."

Her own mention of her recently deceased parents instantly hit Silke as her eyes filled for a moment before she was able to shake it off.

Loraine quickly changed the subject when she noticed Silke's demeanor change. "Wonder how high the creek is?"

"Guess we'll find out pretty soon. It's at the bottom of this ridge," said Bone. "Dollar says they crossed."

"No bet," responded Silke.

Fifteen minutes later they reined up down at the south bank of Wild Horse Creek.

"Tracks lead to the left. Looks like they wanted to cross down there where the water was calmer this side of those rocks…Deeper, but calmer."

"Bone, let's change into our BDUs to cross, looks like the horses will have to swim part way."

"Another good idea, Pard, we can wrap our buckskins in my slicker…keep them dry."

"Oh, right. You mentioned the one drawback about wearing 'em is gettin' wet," said Silke. "Wouldn't be so bad in the summer…would keep you cool, but in winter, it's a horse of another color, I would imagine."

"That is a fact, little missy…We can change over there behind those boulders, Pard," added Bone.

"No foolin' around, ya'll. We don't have time," commented Silke.

"What? Us?" responded Bone.

"Yes, you. Ya'll have only been married two months…I didn't just fall off the watermelon wagon, you know," said Silke with a grin as Bone and Loraine disappeared behind the boulders.

A couple of minutes later, a screech came from behind the big rocks.

"Damn you, Bone, your hands are cold," yelled Loraine.

"Just trying to warm 'em up, Honey Bunch."

"Use your ownself…before I have to hurt you."

Silke shook her head and grinned. Bear Dog looked up at her and cocked his head.

"Don't look at me…I don't want to know what they're doin'."

Loraine, without looking, Gibbs-slapped Bone on the back of his head as they stepped out from the cover of the boulders, knocking his dark green John Bull hat off.

"Ow!" he said as he rubbed his head and picked his hat up from the ground.

"Ya'll are more fun than goin' to one of those vaudeville shows that tours around with games and such for the county fairs."

"It wasn't me, I wasn't there, and I didn't do it," claimed Bone.

"Go to Hell for lying, same as you do for stealing, Bone," said Loraine as she elbowed him in the ribs.

"I wasn't lying...I was just manipulating the truth...like politicians."

"And that makes it all right?"

"Depends on who's listening."

"Well, I'm not a democrat."

"Thank God for small favors," replied Bone.

"Why me, Lord?" Loraine looked up into the fog.

"If ya'll are through with your love makin', you want to cross now?" asked Silke as she stuck her toe in her stirrup and swung up into her saddle.

Bone finished rolling their buckskins and blankets up in his yellow slicker and tied it on behind Hildebrandt's cantle.

Silke dismounted. "That's a good idea, Bone, rolling your blankets in your slickers, too." She pulled hers out and spread it on the ground.

"You might ought to put your chinks in that roll, too," suggested Loraine.

"Ooh, another good idea. Too bad I can't roll Bear Dog up in it too."

"Just put him inside your jacket and button it up," said Bone.

"Dang, ya'll need to fuss more often…Come out with all sorts of good things."

"It's a gift," they said simultaneously.

Silke grinned again, unbuckled her elk hide chinks, laid them along with her blanket on her slicker and rolled it all up. She tied it on top of her saddle bags and then put Bear Dog inside her jacket and buttoned all but the top button. He stuck his head out and licked her chin.

"Yes, I know, Honey, it's warm and cozy in there isn't it?"

He yipped and licked her again as she remounted and led off into the swiftly moving water. As her line-back dun neared to center of the creek he had to begin to swim, forcing Silke to slide out of the saddle and grab the long saddle strings on the front of the left side.

She was then able to roll slightly to her back, to keep Bear Dog's head out of the water as the horse swam through the current to the shallow water near the north bank.

Loraine followed behind her on Sweet Face and mirrored Silke's actions. Bone came right behind her. The big man thought it best to go all the way back to Hildebrandt's long tail to hang on.

As the seventeen hand horse's hooves reached bottom, Bone allowed him to pull his two hundred and eighty-five pounds all the way to knee-deep water before he pulled his legs under him, stood up, and walked out behind his black half Friesian mount.

He waded to shore to join Loraine and Silke. Both were shivering from the cold water and the still nippy air.

"Ladies, we should build a fire to warm up and get a little dried out before we get back on their trail, don't you think?"

Loraine's lips were blue and her teeth chattering as she answered, "Thought you'd never bring it up, Bone."

Twenty minutes later, the three stood close as they could to a roaring fire Bone had built.

"Wearing wet clothing in this weather is a good way to catch the pneumonia, or so my granny said," commented Silke. "Wish I had one of those lighter things you carry, Bone. It's handier than handles on a jug."

Bone turned to warm his backside. "Afraid it's the only one like it in this time period, Silke. I'll have to go to matches when the fuel runs out on this one."

"What does it use?" she asked.

"Butane…It's a byproduct of refining petroleum, crude oil, if you wish. Actually discovered in 1849, but it took years to figure out how to capture it for commercial use. They still burn it off in oil fields…Call it flaring because they don't have a good way to collect it."

"How do you know all that stuff, Bone?" asked Loraine.

He shrugged. "Magic…" Then he grinned. "Plus, I'm a very observant feller."

Bear Dog lay at Silke's feet, occasionally rolling over, enjoying the heat from the flames.

"Reckon that coffee's ready?" asked Silke as she got her cup from her saddle bags which were also close to the fire, drying out.

"If it's not, it oughta be," replied Loraine as she took one of her gloves, picked the blue enameled pot up and filled Silke's proffered cup.

The attractive Pinkerton detective rolled the metal cup with the steaming trail brew between her palms, savoring the heat before she blew across the top, licked the rim, and took a sip.

"I must say, Loraine, you make an outstanding cup of coffee."

"She does that," added Bone. "Say, Silke, what do you make of the way the bank was torn up on this side where we crossed?"

"Looks to me like somebody got in trouble crossing the creek an' had to be rescued."

"Or not," added Loraine. "Maybe they washed on down the creek."

"Don't think so, Loraine. The tracks all had the same depth as before. If someone washed away, one set of the prints would be more shallow."

"Oh, didn't think about that. Wonder who it was?"

"I was getting a real sense of panic from our shooter, Lenny. I'm occasionally picking him up…His vibes are different from the others."

"Vibes? What's that?" asked Silke.

"Short for vibrations…It's a feeling I get about his emotional state because I'm familiar with him from our time…Nothing concrete, just a feeling," answered Bone. "Don't think the little twit can swim."

"What's twit, mean?" she asked.

Bone glanced at Loraine.

"He's a pussy," she grinned and replied to the younger woman.

Silke blushed and put her hand to her mouth. "Oh!"

Bear Dog cocked his head at her.

§§§

CHAPTER EIGHTEEN

FABLE HILLS, IT

"Let's head on into Banner," said Big John. "We kin warm up there an' git some hot chow at Ma's.

"Hey, I heered of Banner. S'pposed to be a hangout fer rustlers an' sech," commented Whitey as they trotted north away from Wild Horse Creek.

"Ain't it up yonder 'tween Wild Horse Creek an' Rush Creek?" asked Duncan.

"Yep, on the edge of Fable Hills…Hid out there a time er two a few years past," added Tackett. "Need some dry supplies anyhoo…The cornmeal, flour an' sugar got soaked…If'n the kid hadn't a panicked, he wouldn't amissed grabbin' his horse's tail."

"He cain't swim," commented Bull.

"His problem," replied Tackett.

Lenny was slumped over in his saddle wrapped in his blanket and slicker. He was shaking with the cold.

"The boy needs to git dry an' warm up, Tackett…Think he's gittin' the chills," said Bull.

"He needs to toughen up, gonna ride with me," replied Big John. "Ain't but five, six miles on up thisaway. He'll be fine…Suck 'em up, boy!"

Lenny didn't respond, he just nodded and pulled the blanket tighter.

Forty minutes later, the gang rode into Banner. It was formerly called Rock Creek, for the feeder creek it sat upon.

"Looks like Ma's is still here," said Tackett as they reined in and dismounted in front of the clapboard building with *MA's EATS* painted across the false front above the canopy.

The gang tied up, stomped their feet on the boardwalk to knock any mud from the street off and followed Big John through the door.

The small twenty-five foot wide cafe was toasty warm from the potbellied stove in the center of the room. The back twenty feet of the fifty foot long building was occupied by the kitchen and storeroom.

A stout woman with mousy salt and pepper hair up in a bun on the back of her head glanced up from wiping a table. "Brought yourselves in, still got some lunch left...Well, Jim Dandy, looky here what the cat drug in...Big John Tackett! Ain't seen you in a month of Sundays...See they ain't hung you yet."

"Hello, Ma. Yore as sassy as ever. Whatcha got to eat?"

Bull directed Lenny over to the glowing red stove. "Stand here, boy...Don't git so close you catch yer blanket on fire. Open it up so's you kin git the heat direct."

"Got Irish stew with plenty taters, corn, tomatoes, and carrots in it, some pot roast left an' some of my special meat loaf…What's yer pleasure?" She glanced over at Lenny. "What's with the youngster, looks a mite peaked."

"Got separated from his horse crossin' Wild Horse…had to haul 'im out on a rope like a noodlin' catfish. Got himself a chill," replied Tackett.

"Then it's the stew fer him…That'll warm 'im up to a fair thee well. How 'bout the rest of you boys?"

"Some of that pot roast an' whatever else you got to go with it fer me," said Big John.

"Take the stew, too, ma'am," added Whitey.

"An' me, Ma," said Duncan.

"Jest as well make it four, plus coffee an' some cornbread…you got it," commented Bull.

"Got plenty cornbread…Hot, too," she replied. "Set yerselves at that table there close to the stove, an' I'll be right back with yer victuals…an' git them hats off." She headed off to the kitchen.

"Warmin' up some, kid?" asked Bull.

Lenny nodded and took a couple of deep breaths.

"Why don't you see as Ma has a sugar tit fer 'im while yer at it?" commented Big John.

Bull turned and glared at Tackett for a long moment.

"Best change yer attitude, there, Waverly. I don't cotton to bein' looked at with the stink eye."

"I'm not overly concerned with what you cotton to, Tackett."

"That's enough," said Ma as she walked up with a tray of their food. "Won't have no shindies in my cafe...You hear me, Big John?"

He looked at her, back to Bull, and then at Ma again and nodded. "Yessum."

She started setting the bowls of stew on the table—the first in front of Lenny, and then the others. Tackett was the last with his plate of pot roast, carrots with smashed potatoes and gravy.

Ma also placed a large basket of steaming cornbread in the center with a bowl of butter from the cooling room below the restaurant.

"Just churned that butter yesterd'y. You boys eat up," she said.

"Oooh-lále, I could make a meal on hot cornbread, butter an' sorghum...Gotn'y buttermilk, Ma?" asked Whitey.

"I do. Bring it right out with the sorghum…'Nbody else?"

"I'll have some of that buttermilk, too, Ma," added J.R. as he tucked his napkin into his collar.

DOUGHERTY, IT

Bass and Padrino finished breakfast and were standing out on the boardwalk in front of Mae's.

Bass looked up at the lifting fog. "Kin almost see the sun. 'Spect fog'll be completely gone in another thirty, forty-five minutes."

"Visibility is up to about three hundred yards, now, I'd say." Padrino glanced down the street in the direction that Walton rode off in.

"I mind Duce'll be easy trackin' in the mud…Let's take the horses down to the livery an' let the hostler give 'em a bait of grain an' a brushin' whilst we…er, you writes up a report fer when the Lighthorse comes through…Needs to git a death certificate from the undertaker on them three bodies, fer the re-ward."

"Not much different in our time," commented Padrino.

"How so?"

"Need to take care of business and do the paperwork."

"Necessary evils…Sometimes you gots to hold yer nose, like takin' medicine…Gots it to do."

They untied their mounts and the pack horse and walked them down the street a short way to Red's Livery.

A middle-aged man with bright red hair sticking out from underneath a battered fedora walked out of the big double doors of the red livery barn.

"Hep ye?" he asked.

"Need to grain an' water the horses. Give 'em a bit of groomin'…We ain't stayin' jest long enough to do some paperwork an' see to gettin' yer local blackmaster to take care of some pariahs what made the mistake of tryin' to hold up the bank."

"That wuz all that shootin' earlier?"

"It was. Both inside and outside the bank," said Padrino.

Red looked at Bass. "You wouldn't be Bass Reeves, would you?"

"What some folks calls me."

"Gosh dang, be an honor to see to yer horses, Marshal…A real honor."

Bass dug in his vest for some silver dollars. "How much you be a needin'?"

"No charge, Marshal, no charge atall. I keep all my money down to that bank. Shore glad ya'll showed up when you did."

"Cain't hardly let you do that, Red...Jest doin' our job...Two dollars cover it?"

"Well, yes, sir, but it would be a pleasure to handle it fer ya'll."

Bass picked up the man's big hand and placed the two Morgans in it. "Ain't gonna discuss it, knows you'll treat 'em good."

Red nodded. "Count on it, Marshal Reeves, count on it."

"We'll be back directly." Bass touched the brim of his hat as he and Padrino turned and headed back down the street toward the bank.

BANNER, IT

Bone, Loraine and Silke trotted their horses down the main street of the small agrarian community. There were only a few citizens about and several horses stood hipshot at the hitching rails in front of Elmore's Mercantile.

"Looks pretty quiet," said Loraine.

"Uh-huh." Bone turned to Silke. "Think they've been here and gone?"

"I would say. Their tracks led to Ma's, but there's no horses there now. Probably ate, warmed up from crossin' the creek and then headed out."

Bone looked around and noticed the name of the mercantile. He grinned big. "Well, what do you know?"

"What?" asked Loraine.

"This is the town they did the movie *Footloose* about."

"No!" exclaimed Loraine.

"What's Footloose," asked Silke.

"You remember us telling you about those motion pictures we have in our time?" Bone glanced at Silke.

"Edison's Kinetoscope?"

"Right...Well, it gets real big in our time with sound, color, and music, and in 1984, they will do a motion picture, entitled *Footloose* about a town that had banned all dancing..."

"Oh, you're funnin'," Silke interrupted. "Not even hootenannys?"

"Especially not hootenannys. Said it was the work of the devil..." Bone grinned and shook his head. "Well, anyway the high school kids decided they'd get around the town ordinance and went outside the city limits and held what's called a prom dance..."

"That basically is a celebration of the end of the school year and the high school graduating class," added Loraine.

"This town will change it's name to Elmore City and will have such an ordnance," said Bone. "The town will also have a saying, 'If the South is the Bible belt...then Elmore City is the buckle.'"

"And this is the town they patterned the movie after?" asked Loraine.

"One in the same."

"It might be because in this time, it's a refuge for outlaws on the scout and rustlers," said Silke.

"Looks like the pendulum will swing all the way in the opposite direction," commented Loraine.

§§§

CHAPTER NINETEEN

WASHITA RIVER

Duce rode west from Dougherty over to the Washita. The fog was slowly lifting as he waded his horse out into the river and soon slid from the saddle and held on to the saddlehorn as his gelding swam toward the other side.

Ken Farmer

The blood bay sloshed ashore and shook violently to remove the excess dripping water. Duce waded out just behind him.

"Damn…Glad I wadn't aboard, old son. You'd a loosened some teeth."

He turned and studied the opposite bank for a long while as his horse cropped the lush winter grass and vetch growing back off the river some twenty feet.

"Don't see nobody, boy. Meby we lost 'em in the fog…whoever in hell they were…Swear an' be damned that old bastard outside was shootin' one of them fast shooters like Lenny has." He looked over at his horse. "Why the hell am I talkin' to you, horse?…Ain't never offered to answer me before."

Duce mused quietly. *Whoever it is, they gotta be tailin' the gang…They wuz damn sure layin' fer us in that bank. Don't believe we'll be ameetin' Big John an' them in Wynnewood after all.*

Duce pulled his boots off, poured the water out of them and managed to stomp them back on. He stabbed a toe in the stirrup and swung into the wet saddle. "God, hate wet boots an' wet saddles more…We'll git up into the Arbuckles, find a gully to build a fire in an' dry out some, boy…I mind you don't like a soggy saddle blanket neither."

He nudged the mustang into a jog trot toward the foothills. *Probably gonna have a rash by the time we git there.*

Several hours later, after Bass and Padrino had taken care of their business in Dougherty with the bodies, they rode up to the east bank of the Washita.

Bass studied where Duce had entered the river and then across to the west bank. He shook his head. "Do believe Mister Walton has done gone an' changed his plans."

"How do you mean?" asked Padrino.

"All the time we been atrackin' him an' the others, they been steady headin' north…now, he done cut back to the west after losin' his men."

"Think he's striking out on his own and not going to meet back up with the others?"

Bass turned to Padrino. "Exactly what I thinks…Knows somebody's on his tail."

He took his old briarwood pipe from his vest, loaded it with his maple flavored tobacco and lit it with a waxed strike-anywhere match from the same pocket. Bass took a long draw and pondered a moment or two as was his long time habit when he had to make a decision. He finally exhaled a blue cloud over his head.

"Purty smart fer a malefactor. Usually theys dumb as a bucket of rocks…Why they be fair easy to catch, most of the time."

He glanced back over at Padrino and nodded. "Tackett's with the other bunch. He's the one I gots paper on…We go north an' jine back up with Bone an' them…Git Duce 'nother time."

"Going after the head of the snake, then?" questioned Padrino.

"Uh-huh."

CHICKASAW NATION

Big John and his bunch had ridden out of Banner after stocking up on their supplies at Elmore's Mercantile.

"We're 'bout fifteen miles er so from Wynnewood. Duce an' them should already be there, they didn't have as far to go as us," said

Tackett. "If they ain't, not 'bout to wait on 'em...we go on an' haul ass to Oklahoma City."

"Gotta cross the river, don't we?" asked Duncan.

"Do, but there's a chain barge ferry 'tween here an' there...er was. Baby sister won't be gittin' her toes wet this time."

"That ain't called for, Tackett," said Bull who was riding alongside Lenny.

"Call 'em like I sees 'em."

Waverly glanced at Lenny. He was still not feeling up to par. "You awright, kid?"

"I'll make it...Still a bit chilled. It'll pass," Lenny replied.

BANNER, IT

Bone, Loraine and Silke tied up in front of Ma's and went inside.

"Come right in an' find yerself a seat. Got some left now that the rush is over," said Ma when she heard the bell over the door tinkle.

Bone and Silke hung their hats on the pegs and pulled out chairs at a table near the stove and sat down.

"What'll it be? Got Irish stew or you can have Irish stew." Ma grinned.

Bone returned her grin as he glanced at Loraine and then Silke. "Believe I'll have the Irish stew...Ya'll?"

"Oh, let's see...Think I'll try the Irish stew, also," replied Loraine.

"Well, guess that's what I'll have, too...if coffee comes with it?" added Silke. "Oh, could I have a small bowl for my friend?" She unbuttoned her jacket, took Bear Dog out and set him on the floor.

"I think we can work that out...Ain't he cute." Ma looked at each one of them. "Ya'll law?"

"How can you tell?" asked Bone.

"Oh, honey, been runnin' this cafe for a lotta years...Seen 'em all, robbers, killers, rustlers, outlaws on the scout, deserters...an' law dogs. Can usually pick 'em when they walk in the door...After Big John?"

"Could say that," said Silke. "Killed nine people in the last few days, that we know about...includin' my momma and daddy down in Texas."

"Oh, sweetheart, I'm so sorry to hear that. Big John's a mean one...He don't need catchin'...he needs a killin'."

"Been here, I guess?" asked Loraine.

"Few hours back...Warmed up, ate an' headed east...One of 'em seemed a mite puny. Youngest of the bunch...Chilled to the bone, he was."

Bone and Loraine looked at each other.

"Lenny," said the big man. "Bet he's the one they had to pull out of the river."

"No bet," answered Loraine.

"Be right back with your stew an' coffee, folks," said Ma as she turned and headed for the kitchen.

Loraine glanced over at Silke. "What's to the east?"

"The Washita River then Wynnewood...There's a ferry 'cross the river there."

"Bet they're headed that way," said Bone.

PRICE, IT

Bass and Padrino rode up to the tower where the Gulf and Colorado Railroad would fill up her tank.

The jerkwater stop was almost eighty miles from the last water tank at Gainesville. Price was too small to have a regular train station.

"What time did the station attendant back in Dougherty say the northbound would be stopping for water?" asked Padrino.

Bass pulled his silver pocket watch from his vest, popped the cover and checked the time. "'Bout thirty minutes from now…she's on time."

The two men dismounted, loosened the girths on their horses and looked off to the south.

"Don't see any smoke yet…You said it was about twenty miles to Wynnewood from here."

"Uh-huh. Kin be there in 'round a half-hour 'stead of four hours by horseback…Shore save wear an' tear on the boys," answered Bass. "If'n they gots a stock car."

"Usually do, don't they?"

"Most always…lessen it be a express run."

Padrino glanced south again. "Smoke."

"She be right on time," said Bass.

Ten minutes later the locomotive blew steam as it coasted up to the steel water tower. The engineer maneuvered the fuel and water tender underneath the spigot.

The boilerman climbed on top of the tender, opened the water hatch, pulled the spigot down and jerked the chain. The water gushed from the eight inch diameter pipe with the canvas sleeve at the mouth into the large water storage tank in the tender and in several minutes, had filled it back up.

Bass and Padrino rode up to the cab of the locomotive to address the engineer.

"Howdo, I be Deputy US Marshal Bass Reeves an' we be needin' to catch a ride up to Wynnewood, you don't mind."

"Bass Reeves? I'll be danged...Shore, be right proud to give you a lift, Marshal...Conductor's name is Vergil an' I see him walkin' thisaway, now. He'll git ya'll loaded up...Verg, this here is Marshal Bass Reeves. They need a ride up to Wynnewood."

"Recognized you right off, Marshal, when ya'll rode up...You've ridden with us a time or two. Ya'll foller me back down to the stock car an' I'll lower the ramp."

"'Preciate it, Vergil, this is Posseman..." He turned to Padrino. "Say, what's yer real name? Knows you jest goes by Padrino, but that ain't what yer mamma called you."

Padrino grinned and nodded. "No, my Christian name is Jethro Barthelomew Pereira. But, she only called me that when I was in trouble."

Bass whistled. "That be a mouthful, believe we'll jest stick with Padrino…ain't sure I kin say all that other, anyhoo." He turned back to the conductor. "Lead on, Vergil."

The blue-clad railroad employee turned around and headed back down the train to the stock car just past the last passenger car.

He unlatched the ramp which also served as the wide door on the side of the car, and Bass helped him lower it to the ground.

Padrino had already dismounted and led Star and Bart up the cleated ramp inside the car. He tied them off on one of the side rails alongside a couple of other horses already onboard as Bass led Flash inside.

Padrino and Bass jumped to the ground and helped Vergil pull the ramp back up in place where the conductor latched it.

There's some seats in this last passenger car, Marshal."

"Much obliged," replied Bass as he and Padrino walked the short distance to the steps at the rear of the car and boarded.

Vergil waved toward the cab that all was ready. The engineer released the Johnson bar and the locomotive chugged away from the tower and gained speed in the short run across the bucolic countryside of the Chickasaw Nation to Wynnewood...

§§§

CHAPTER TWENTY

WASHITA RIVER

Big John led the men onto the ferry. They dismounted and held their mount's reins.

"Welcome 'board…Name's Charlie. Be a dollar an' a quarter fer the five of ya an' yer horses."

"Don't think so," said Tackett as he pulled his .45 and stuck it in the man's face. "Let's say that today this trip is on the house...Get my meanin', old timer?"

The crusty old riverman looked down the barrel of the Colt and then spat a long stream of tobacco into the muddy water of the river.

"Uh...See what you mean...may have a point there...Uh, ya'll hang on tight."

He put the big windlass and cathead connected to the small steam engine mounted amidships in gear and the ferry slowly crept out into the current, the thick chain clattered as it wound around the cathead.

Ten minutes later, the nose of the barge bumped onto the eastern shore at the base of the chain anchor.

The gang led their horses off the ferry and mounted up.

Tackett turned his mount facing the barge and the ferryman, Charlie. "Well, much obliged, old man, and jest in case there's anybody comin' up behind us, we would appreciate it if'n you'd not bring 'em across."

"That ain't no problem, sir. Why, I'll jest sit rightchere the rest of the day."

"I know," responded Big John as he drew his Colt and shot Charlie.

The wizened old ferryman grasped his chest, looked at the outlaw leader with confusion for a brief moment, and then collapsed to the deck like so much wet newspaper.

Bull and Lenny both glared at Tackett and shook their heads while Whitey and J.R. were nonplused.

Big John laughed, reined his horse to the east and spurred him off. The others dutifully followed.

They quickly rode the short five miles into Wynnewood.

"We'll go to Maude's Parlor House. One of my favorite places here in the territory…Duce an' the others will meet us there…Give 'em two hours."

WASHITA RIVER

Bone, Loraine, and Silke pulled up at the ferry station on the west side of the river over two hours since the Tackett gang had crossed.

"Well, ferry's on the other side. Guess we'll have to wait till old Charlie brings her back across," said Silke.

"Don't see anyone on board," commented Loraine.

Bone pulled out his new set of binoculars and zeroed in on the chain barge. "Uh-oh."

"What is it?" asked Silke.

He handed her the binoculars. "Body laying on the deck...That him?"

Silke focused on the body. "Oh, no...That's Charlie all right. Always wears bib overalls an' a red an' white-checked shirt...The way he's layin', he's either had a heart attack..." She looked over at Bone and Loraine. "...or been shot."

"Still some smoke coming from the boiler. Hasn't been there too long."

Bone dismounted, hung his John Bull hat and gun belt on his saddle horn and pulled his buckskin shirt over his head. He sat down on the ground, unlaced his tall Apache-style moccasins and pulled them off, then he got to his feet, dropped his pants and stood beside Hildebrandt in his white skivvies.

"I apologize, Silke."

"No worry. Seen my Pa in his drawers many times. Take it you're gonna swim across."

He nodded. "No need in gettin' everything wet again. Did this many times as a Recon Marine."

"What are you going to do when you get over there?" asked Loraine.

"That steam engine is still hot. Check the pressure and bring her back across."

"Ever run a steam engine before?" asked Silke.

"Nope...How hard can it be. Barge can only go two directions."

"You say so," Silke responded.

Bone walked upstream about fifty yards and waded out into the icy water.

"Why're you going up there, Bone?" yelled Silke.

"Current will carry me back down to the ferry," he hollered back.

"Ah, I see," she yelled again.

"Oh, good God in Heaven," he said as he got crotch deep in the current.

"Hope you don't need to pee, Honey," commented Loraine as she raised her voice to be heard.

He looked back at her and hollered, "You kiddin'. Couldn't find it if I did."

"That's what I was talking about." Loraine giggled.

Bone submerged to get wet all over, then surfaced and struck out using a powerful breast stroke and angled toward the center of the seventy yard wide river.

It looked as if Bone was swimming in a large arc as the strong current carried him back in line with the ferry as he predicted.

A large uprooted tree from the recent storm was being carried by the current downstream, directly in line to Bone.

"Look out!" Loraine and Silke screamed together.

Bone disappeared under the big tree.

Loraine and Silke grabbed each other as they watched in horror.

The huge piece of flotsam continued on down the river.

Loraine and Silke studied the roiling water around and behind the tree, concern was written plainly on their faces.

In what seemed like long minutes later, Bone's head popped to the surface five yards downstream and on the far side of the tree as he continued stroking to the far bank.

Loraine and Silke both breathed a sigh of relief as they glanced at each other.

"Only Bone," whispered Loraine.

He reached the other side just ten feet downstream from the ferry, waded up on shore, shook like a wet dog, walked back up to it and stepped aboard.

Bone checked Charlie's pulse and raised his eyelids. He looked across the river and shook his head. He got to his feet, walked over to the steam boiler and checked the pressure. He remained close to the firebox warming up for a moment before moving over to the wood pile.

Bone glanced up as he heard the hoofbeats of trotting horses coming up to the ferry from the east.

"You in the habit of wanderin' 'round in yer drawers, Bone?" asked Bass Reeves.

"Around the house, yeah, but out here in the boonies?...Is this a new chapter for you, Bone?" added Padrino.

Both men had big grins across their faces until they saw Charlie's body.

"Gosh dang o'mighty," said Bass as he dismounted, ground tied Flash, and ran aboard.

He knelt beside Charlie and then looked up at Bone. "Tackett?"

"My guess, Bass. Probably trying to keep us from following." Bone pointed across the river. "Couldn't see any point in all of us gettin' wet."

Padrino had dismounted also, pulled a blanket from one of the panniers, brought it on board and draped it over his godson's broad shoulders.

"Thanks, Padrino. Is a mite chilly."

"I was making a wild guess when I saw the size of your goose bumps," he replied.

"Well, let's fire this boat up an' back across the river to git the ladies," commented Bass as he knocked the iron locking dog holding the door to the fire box closed and opened it with a poker.

Padrino grabbed a couple of split oak logs and pitched them inside. Bass picked up two more to add, and then closed and latched the door back.

"Be pressured up in a few minutes," said the Marshal.

"I'll stay over here and get a fire going. I expect you'd like one," offered Padrino.

"You think?" Bone turned to Bass. "Know how to operate this thing?"

"Oh, shore. Used to work on one 'cross the Arkansas 'fore I got my commission."

"Good thing. I was going to have to do it by gosh an' by golly an' hope I didn't blow the dang thing up," said Bone.

Bass looked at the gauge. "I mind ol' Charlie had already set the relief valve when he started the run...Awrighty then, she's ready."

He grabbed the long handle similar to a Johnson bar on a locomotive and threw it into gear. The engine shuddered and then started winding the two inch chain around the cathead with a rattle, pulling the barge away from the shore and toward the other side.

Ten minutes later, same as when the Tackett gang crossed in the other direction, the ferry bumped at the dock landing by the chain anchor point on the west bank.

"See you picked up some passengers, Bone," said Loraine as she let the short gate down at the end of the barge.

She and Silke led their horses aboard and gave Bass a hug respectively.

"Guess you want your clothes back, Bone?...Or you just going to stand around half naked in your underwear all day for us to gawk at?" Loraine gave her husband a hug also.

"Well, if I have my druthers, believe I'd like to have my duds back. Notwithstanding the blanket Padrino gave me, I'm about to freeze to death...Hey, ya'll know the difference between naked and neked, don't you?"

"Naked an' neked?...Well, guess not," replied Silke.

"Here we go," said Loraine.

Bone grinned as he started pulling on his buckskin pants. "Naked means...you don't have any clothes on...and neked means...you don't have any clothes on...and you're up to somethin'." He giggled.

"Damn you, Bone," said Loraine as she Gibbs slapped him behind the head. "That's almost as bad as the one you pulled on me back home that time about chicken and a blanket."

"Excuse me?" asked Silke.

Bone looked at her with his enigmatic grin. "You know the difference between a plate of chicken and sex on a blanket?"

"Oh, boy, no…and I'm afraid to ask," replied Silke.

"Wanna go on a picnic?"

Loraine backhanded him across his chest while Silke laughed.

Bear Dog stuck his head out of her jacket to see what all the racket was about.

"What's you gots there, Silke?" asked Bass.

"Found a friend at a farm a ways back. Tackett an' them killed the man an' his wife just like my folks an' this little fellow was in the barn."

"Wolf-dog, ain't he?"

"I think so," she replied.

"Gots a name yet?" Bass asked.

"Bear Dog."

"Fits 'im…Look at them blue eyes. Don't believe I ever seen a blue-eyed wolf-dog…Jack's is gots gold eyes."

"Bet one of his parents was either border collie…"

"Er a catahoula…They be from Louisiana. Use 'em to hunt wild hogs an' cattle in the swamps. Gots me one to home. Calls him Buttercup on accounts of he be yeller an' black with blue eyes…Damn good dogs…Smarts too," said Bass. "Gotta watch 'em though…They don'ts know when to back down…Had to hold Buttercup onct from attackin' a full-growed panther," said Bass as he threw the bar into gear to go back across the river.

Bear Dog yipped and squirmed to get down as the ferry chugged away from the west bank. Silke set him on the deck. He went immediately to Bass, sniffed of him, set down, cocked his head and lifted one paw.

"Believe he likes you, Bass," commented Bone as he continued to dress, pulling his soft buckskin shirt over his head.

"Dogs most does. Awlays says, best pays 'tention if'n a dog don't like somebody…They's usually a purty good reason."

Bear Dog yipped again…

§§§

CHAPTER TWENTY-ONE

WYNNEWOOD, IT

The Tackett gang reined up outside a yellow
two-story clapboard building with a full, across the
front, balcony. A red hand-painted ornate sign over
the fancy carved wood and frosted glass door at the
entrance said *MAUDE'S PARLOR HOUSE.*

They dismounted at the hitching rails alongside several other horses, all standing hipshot.

"How is it you know Maude, Big John?" asked Whitey.

The big man chuckled. "Oh, I've visited her a time er two over the years...I kinda Think she likes what I bring to the table." He spat an amber stream of viscous tobacco juice to the dirt street beside his horse as he led him over to the water trough to slake his thirst.

The others led their mounts to the trough as well, and then they all loosened their girths, tied up and went inside after stomping their boots on the porch welcome mat to knock any mud off.

"Well, well, the prodigal son returneth," said a buxom bleached-blond in a low-cut full length satin dress. "What brings you to our fair city, Big John?...On the scout or the dodge?"

"Blam-jam, Maude you always like to clean my plow, don'tcha?" replied Big John.

"Oh, I 'spect we'll be doin' that before you leave. How much time you got?"

"Couple hours, I reckon...Waitin' on some fellers."

She chuckled, drew on the long brown cigarillo in a bone holder between her fingers and blew a blue smoke ring over her head. "I doubt you or your boys'll last that long anyway…'Specially the puppy there."

"You can leave me out, ma'am, I'll just have a drink. If that's all right?"

Big John and the others turned and stared at Lenny.

Maude grinned and nodded. "Don't like the ladies, that it?"

Lenny quickly blushed. "Uh, no, ma'am…I mean yes, ma'am. Uh…I mean I'm just not in the mood."

Maude looked at him with a twinkle in her eye. "Uh-huh…Not kiddin' me, honey. Been in this business too long…Seen it all. Know the look." She glanced at Big John who had a puzzled expression on his face and then back at Lenny. "Got a young boy upstairs might suit you."

Lenny had a panic look cross his face as he glanced at Big John, the others, and finally Bull. "That's all right, ma'am, just have a drink is all. I'm feelin' a little poorly."

"I understand, honey, I understand…Just see that colored fellow over there, he'll fix you up with a drink," she said with a wink. "The rest of you follow me."

The others followed the madam with a final last look at Lenny.

WASHITA RIVER

The ferry bumped ashore and Bass lowered the railing at the ramp.

Bone, Loraine and Silke led their mounts off while Bass closed all the dampers on the steam engine fire box to kill the fire.

"Has to send the coroner out to see 'bout pore ol' Charlie's body. Don't know as they's anybody what kin take over the ferry, but, I mind somebody will."

Bear Dog padded to the front and jumped the final six inches to the shore, promptly ran over and watered a dogwood sapling. Then he started sniffing around at all the new scents before he darted over to Padrino whcrc hc was tending the fire.

The white-haired retired Marine bent over and scratched the pup's ears. Bear Dog promptly fell over and rolled to his back for a belly rub. He was rewarded.

"Well, see that you too have passed the Bear Dog test," said Silke.

"That's the same thing our dog, Tyrin, back home does…exactly. Interesting," commented Padrino.

"Coffee ready?" asked Bass.

"Is if ya'll are," Padrino replied.

Bone stepped over, after ground tying Hildebrandt on some yellow hop clover nearby, holding out two blue swirl graniteware cups—one for him, the other for Loraine.

Bone turned to Bass. "So, where's your bunch?"

"Dead…all but one, that is."

"What happened?" asked Silke as she sat down on a nearby log with her cup.

Bear Dog had tired of sniffing around after meeting everyone, collapsed at Silke's feet and promptly fell asleep.

Ten minutes later, Bass and Padrino finished going through the attempted bank robbery at Dougherty, IT.

"So, that's purty much the name of that tune. Fer as we could tell, Duce Walton lit out west fer the Oklahoma Territory...Think he figured out they wuz bein' tailed an' wuzn't havin' none of it," said Bass.

He blew across the top of his coffee, licked the rim, took a sip of the hot trail brew and looked at Silke. "How far behind Tackett and the others you reckon ya'll are?"

"Not far, Bass." She drank a bit from her own cup. "They had lunch at Ma's in Banner about two hours before we did."

"I took it that the ferry operator had been dead at least that long when ya'll rode up. Rigor mortis hadn't completely set in. Just the eyelids, face and jaw were in full, the larger muscles were just partial...Considering the ambient temperature, full body rigor mortis should occur about four hours after death...'Course no way to tell how long Charlie held on after he was shot," said Bone.

"There was a lot of congealed blood around and under the body, so it looked like he bled out fairly quickly," added Loraine.

Bass looked Padrino. "What'd they say?"

"Charlie had been dead about two hours when we got there," Padrino replied.

He looked back at Bone. "Why didn't you jest say so?"

Bone and Loraine exchanged glances.

"Thought we did," replied Loraine. She glanced back a Bone. "Should have gotten the thermometer out of our crime kit and taken his temp."

"Yeah, coulda, shoulda, woulda…I was freezin' my ass off when Bass and Padrino rode up and our kit was with you."

"What's this 'kit' ya'll er talkin' 'bout?"

"In our time we have what we call a Crime Scene Investigation kit, Silke. We can check for fingerprints, blood or semen or gunshot residue…check for time of death, things like that. It's for the collection of evidence for any trial," said Loraine.

"We made one to use in this time with what we have to work with. If some perpetrator tries to cover up a crime scene, say by washing to hide blood stains...even with bleach, we can find it."

"Yer funnin' me."

"Kid you not, Bass. Comes in kind of handy when some killer or rapist tries to...say, 'It wasn't me, I wasn't there and I didn't do it'."

"Thought that was your line, Bone?" commented Silke with a grin.

He grinned back. "Well it is, but just for jokes and fun."

"No, it's true, Bass. It's amazing how much they can find at a crime scene that the person that committed it never thinks about...especially fingerprints, hairs, fibers, and DNA," added Padrino.

"What be DNA?"

"Nothing to worry about, Bass. Won't have that for almost another sixty years. But, we can check for fingerprints...No two people in the world have the same prints...Not even twins," said Loraine.

"That's interestin'. Do you suppose you could make me one of those kits when we finish this?" asked Silke.

"I would imagine," replied Bone, glancing at Loraine.

"Bunches of the time, it ain't necessary, when the malefactor decides they doesn't wants to come in...peaceable like," said Bass. "Ain't no need for evidence when they ain't no trial."

Bone nodded. "Even in our time, there's always a few of those who want to commit suicide by cop."

"How many felony warrants have you served in your...what?...Twenty-five years of service?"

"Closter to twenty-four, Silke...so fer, an' Judge Parker issued around nine thousand felony warrants in his twenty years on the bench...an' reckon I served purt near three thousand of 'em," said Bass.

"Good gosh all mighty," exclaimed Loraine. "I didn't know that."

"Ain't never hads one I didn't serve...yet. If'n I gots paper, comes hell er high water, I'm gonna track 'em down. The law ain't ever thing to me...It's the only thing...Without laws, we jest as well go back to livin' in caves an' trees."

"How many have you had to kill in the line of duty?" asked Silke.

"Best as I kin figger...'countin' earlier today...been thirteen to date." He grinned his big toothy smile. "'Course ain't over yet. Never kilt nobody what didn't need killin'...or to keep from killin' me."

"Well, what say we get on the trail on over to Wynnewood and see if Big John's group went through there...There's one that definitely needs killing," said Bone.

"Same goes for Lenny, in my opinion," added Loraine. "He's already been sentenced to twenty years to life...should have gotten a lethal injection execution."

Silke looked at Bone and then at Bass. "Just so there's no misunderstandin'...He's mine," she hissed.

She glanced at Bone's S&W 500, .50 cal on his hip. "Just wish I had a gun like Bone's...Put a hole in him big enough to drive a six-up stagecoach through."

Bone grinned. "Maybe come time when we catch up to 'em, Silke...We can work something out."

§§§

CHAPTER TWENTY-TWO

WYNNEWOOD, IT

Bull hung back as the others followed Maude into the parlor behind the heavy velour burgundy drapes. He turned, walked back to Lenny and sat down on the dark green settee in the foyer next to him. The colored porter handed Lenny a sour-mash whiskey.

He turned to Bull. "Will they be anythin' fer you, suh?

"Red eye."

"Yassuh." The black man disappeared through some identical draperies at the side of the foyer.

"Don't worry about it kid…" Bull looked around. "About bein' a batty boy an' all."

Lenny got a puzzled expression on his face. "What's a batty boy?"

Weatherly lowered his voice. "You know, a bender…a Nancy…a friend of Dorothy?"

"Huh?…Oh. You mean a homosexual?"

"Uh…Yeah…I been known to be a moffie myself…on occasion."

"Really?"

Bull looked at the floor, nodded and said softly, "Whole lot less trouble sometimes than dealin' with a woman."

It was Lenny's turn to glance around. "Right about that."

The porter reentered with Bull's rye on a tray. "Here you is, suh. Be 'nythin' else I kin do fer ya?"

"This is fine," Bull replied.

The porter went back through the drapes.

"I take it that Big John doesn't like…uh…Nancys?" commented Lenny.

"Big John don't like nothin' er nobody…He's a vile man with no soul."

"I thought he liked me…there at first," said Lenny.

"He likes that shooter you got…Why I been takin' up for you…Watchin' yer back. He's a real backshootin', sidewinder, don't give a tunk who it is, neither."

Lenny took a healthy swig of his sour mash and Bull followed suit.

An hour later Whitey and J.R. came back through the drapes to the parlor with satisfied looks across their faces. Each carried a glass of whiskey.

"By the Lord Harry, there wadn't no slack in that little gal's rope," said Whitey.

"Same with mine or God's a possum," replied J.R."

"Uh-huh, could throw my hat over a windmill," added Whitey.

J.R. looked at Lenny and Bull. "Ya'll already done too?"

"Yeah, jest waitin' on the rest of ya'll," replied Bull.

Big John came through the drapes accompanied by Maude.

"Well, you be sure to come see me next time you're through this way...when you have more time," she said as she gave him a big hug.

Tackett swatted her ample bottom and turned to his men. "Let's head north boys. Don't need to stay in one place too long...ain't healthy. I'm thinkin' Duce an' them ain't gonna show."

WASHITA RIVER

Padrino kicked dirt on the fire and poured what was left of the coffee on top.

Silke had loosened her girth enough to reach under the saddle and pull a bubble in the blanket underneath the gullet to keep the saddle from pinching *Lakná's* withers. She tightened the cinch back up, shook the saddle back and forth to settle it, stuck her toe in her two inch leather-wrapped wood stirrup and swung into the saddle.

Bear Dog lay between her thighs, behind the pommel, his head rested on her right leg.

Silke led out on the narrow wagon road east to Wynnewood. Bone rode a little behind her with Loraine at his side.

Bass and Padrino followed them with the pack horse.

Bone studied the road. "Lenny's still with them, no question," he said as he pointed at the straight-sided mule type rear shoes almost at the back of the group. "Silke, you're better at this than I am…How many are we following?"

"Still five, Bone."

"Tracks look fair fresh, too, Silke," said Bass from behind.

"Was thinkin' the same thing, Bass…Two hours…Maybe less."

"I'd say," Bass replied. "Red Wolf done teached you good."

"Still learnin', though," she said.

"We all is, Silke, we all is."

"I saw a quote from that western writer in our time, Ken Farmer, from what he called his Ponderings. It went…'You know, it's what we learn after we think we know it all that actually counts'," commented Padrino.

Bass chuckled. "Ain't that the truth…I likes to say don't never pass up a good opportunity to jest sit a while an' ponder."

"You got any words of wisdom, Loraine?" asked Silke.

She nodded. "My favorite…and this applies to our work in law enforcement is…'When you deal with stupidity, you'll find it has no limits'."

"Ooh, good one. My daddy always said…'There ain't no standin' still, girl, you're either gettin' better…or you're gettin' worse'," said Silke.

She glanced over at Bone. "Well?"

Bone paused for a moment. "In any moment of decision or crises, the first thing you think of to do is usually the right thing…the next thing you think of is usually the wrong thing…but the worst thing you can do…is nothing." He smiled. "Bone's enigma."

They all thought for a minute and then nodded as they rode into the edge of Wynnewood.

Bass held up his big hand for all to stop. "Looky yonder they's quite a few horses in front of Maude's Parlor House."

"Parlor House? Is that a broth…"

Bone interrupted Loraine. "You're right on, Pard. No saloons in the Nations durin' this time period before statehood. So, they had parlor houses with brothels that you could get alcohol and visit girls of the line."

"Girls of the line?" questioned Loraine.

"Painted Ladies, fallen angels, sportin' gals, whor…"

"Oh, got it," Loraine interrupted Silke back.

"I mind we dismount an' ties up back down here…Gots me a feelin' that meby them is our boys makin' a quick stop."

They reined over, tied up in front of a millenary shop and a bakery and dismounted.

"Best not loosen yer girths in case we gots to go to a tail chase real fast."

"What are you going to do with Bear Dog, Silke?" asked Loraine.

"This." She unbuckled one side of her saddlebags, set the pup in with his head and front paws sticking out. "Stay there, Bear Dog."

The pup started to whine, but Silke held up a finger and wagged it in front of his face. "Ah-ah." She kissed the top of his head.

He immediately stopped and just watched her step over to Bone. "Wanna trade irons for a little bit?"

He arched his eyebrows as he pulled his Smith & Wesson from the holster. "Remember, kicks like a mule and only holds five rounds." He removed some extra .50 cal cartridges from his belt and handed them to her also.

Silke handed him her .38-40, but he shook his head as she put the extra rounds in her jean jacket pocket.

"Got a Remington .44 in my saddlebag, you keep yours in case you get in a tight."

She looked up at the big man, grinned and nodded. "Not likely."

"Gonna stick it in your belt?" asked Bone.

Silke shook her head. "Just gonna carry it. Not used to drawin' it...Might drop the big sonofabuck."

Bone grinned. "You got small hands...Use both of them when you fire."

She nodded.

"Let's spread out. Ain't no tellin' when they a gonna come out," said Bass.

"Red alert!" said Loraine. "Door's opening."

"Let's take cover so they don't see us. Be hell to play if we have to dig them out of that building...Too many innocents," commented Bone.

They scattered to cover in door entries and an alleyway.

"Well, by James, feels good to git yer pipes cleaned, don't it?" Tackett slapped Whitey on the back as they split up and headed to their mounts.

"Big John Tackett! This is Marshal Bass Reeves. I gots paper on you. Give it up...We gots you surrounded," Bass shouted from directly across the street as he stepped out from the alley.

Tackett turned, spied Bass and drew his gun. "The hell you say, nigger."

He snapped a hurried shot at the marshal, missing, but the round ricocheted from the brick bank building to Bass' right and whined off in the distance. The sound of the gunshot and ricochet frightened a horse tethered near the black man.

The animal jerked, snapping the reins tied to a hitch rail, spun around and knocked Bass to the dirt street as it galloped off in a panic.

The other outlaws, except Bull and Lenny scattered for cover.

Bass had ducked just before getting knocked down when Big John fired, but saw Bull holding up his hands.

"I give Marshal! I give!" He unbuckled his gun belt and let it drop to the boardwalk.

Bone fired his Remington at Whitey who was drawing a bead on a vulnerable Bass Reeves. The .44 cal bullet struck him in the middle of the chest with a thwack, staggering the man back against the side of Maude's. He slowly slid down the yellow wall, leaving a six inch wide smear of blood.

J.R. took cover behind the watertrough and raised up to shoot at Bone.

Loraine snapped off three quick rounds from her Kimber 1911A that sounded like one, at the outlaw. Two rounds impacted him in the center of his chest and the third in the middle of his forehead.

Lenny looked across the street at Bone. "What the hell are you doin' here?"

"Ask you the same thing, worm," replied Bone.

Duncan spun around from Loraine's shots and fell backward into the trough—his lower legs were left outside and draped over the edge as the water inside began to turn red.

Tackett was distracted from Bass by Bull surrendering to his left. He turned on the heavyset man. "Damn you to hell, you an' the pansy ain't about to give up."

Big John thumbed two rounds at Weatherly, one catching him in the stomach and the other at the base of the throat spraying blood out the back of his neck when it passed through.

Bull collapsed into Lenny, taking them both to the boardwalk.

"Bull! Bull!" Lenny screamed as he squirmed out from under the bigger man and then fell on top of him. "No! No, Bull! Don't die, please," he cried.

Silke stepped out from a doorway and started walking coolly straight toward Tackett. Her right hand was behind her back, the left at her side.

A surprised Big John turned to face her, his Colt pointed at her chest. "Hold it! I got the gun, woman."

She never slowed as she brought the hand holding Bone's 500 out from behind her back. "No, *this* is a gun." Silke brought it up to eye level with both hands and thumbed the hammer back.

At the same time, Lenny got to his feet from beside Bull, drew and aimed his Colt .45 semiautomatic at Tackett. "You killed him! He was my friend. Damn you all to hell!" He squeezed the trigger as fast as he could, firing three rounds.

Silke smiled, her blue eyes took on a flinty look as she also pulled the trigger on the .50 cal.

The simultaneous gunfire created an ear piercing roar as the three .45s and one .50 caliber bullet all struck Tackett in the center of the chest creating a massive red cloud in front and behind the outlaw.

Big John was blasted back two steps where he crumpled to the boardwalk like a pile of wet spaghetti being dropped from a two-story building—dead when he landed.

The sudden silence was deafening as Bone, Loraine, Padrino and Bass turned their eyes to Silke standing in the middle of the street—the 500 still pointed in Tackett's direction.

They all looked to where Lenny had been—he was gone. Only a pile of crumpled clothing and a hat remained where he had stood less than twenty seconds before…

§§§

EPILOGUE

WYNNEWOOD, IT

Bone, Loraine, Bass, and Silke stood over the pile of clothing and hat that was Lenny Taylor as Padrino walked up.

"Darn, my view of the gang was blocked by some hitched horses. By the time I could get a clear shot...it was over." He shook his head. "Shades of the OK Corral, the whole thing lasted about thirty to thirty-five seconds...What the hell happened here?" asked Padrino. "Is...or was that Lenny?"

Bone nodded. "Guess we have an answer to the temporal enigma, or paradox question. Better known as the grandfather paradox."

"What's the grandfather paradox?" asked Silke.

"Lenny was from our time and apparently, unbeknownst to Lenny, Big John was most likely his great or great, great grandfather. The temporal paradox was always the question of what would happen if you went back in time and killed your own grandfather..."

"Lenny ceased to exist. Even the gun he brought from our time and used is gone," Loraine interrupted Bone.

Padrino knelt down and felt through the clothing and pulled a round flat, blue crystal stone with two reverse half-moons and other angular carvings in the center. He held the silver dollar sized stone up to the light.

"Most likely blue quartz or maybe even sapphire," he said. "Think we found the key on how he got here. This is known as the enigma symbol. Been seen all over the world in those crop circle things, petroglyphs and elsewhere." He handed it to Bone. "Here, feel…it's warm like my *moldivite* crystal."

"It's a power crystal. Wonder if he came through our cave or another portal?" asked Bone.

"I suspect that's one of those questions we'll never have an answer to," said Padrino.

"Why is that still here?" asked Silke.

Padrino turned to her. "Because it's probably been here on this planet for a few thousand years…preceeding Lenny finding and using it. Existed long before he did…Maybe Lucy can add something to this when we get back to the house."

"Now this be strange, too," said Bass as he knelt down beside Big John's body.

"What's that?" asked Loraine as she stepped over also.

"Ain't but one bullet hole in his chest, the big one from Silke…an' I knows I seen that kid shoot three bullets in him," said Bass.

"That's because it was the .50 cal from Bone's gun that Silke put in him that was the killing shot. In any event…the second her shot blew through his heart…Lenny just never existed…so he never fired any shots," replied Bone.

Bass shook his head. "Jest don't understands all this. Makes my head hurt."

"No one really has an answer, Bass. Like Lucy said, 'the best minds on two worlds can't figure this time travel thing out'...All we know is that Lenny was here, Silke killed his direct ancestor...and he just plain ceased to exist...it's like he never was," said Padrino.

"That's why it's called the temporal paradox or enigma," said Bone.

"It's fairly late, lets see if Stella and Peach are at the ranch close to the statue," commented Padrino as he pulled out his Galaxy cell phone, held the enigma crystal against it, hit the speed dial number for Peach and put it on speaker.

It rang several times and Peach answered with her deep Georgia accent. "Padrino, Padrino, Padrino, that you, sweet pea?"

BONE'S RANCH - 2019

Peach and Stella were sitting at the kitchen table directly over the cellar where the statue was at Bone's ranch, having a late afternoon beer.

She had answered her cell, quickly put it on speaker and laid it flat on the table.

Padrino's voice came through, "Hang on, let me check…Yep, it's me."

"Oh, bless your sweet heart, quit bein' ugly…Know where Bone gets it. Ya'll awright?…We really miss you," she asked.

Tyrin started bouncing up and down on his front feet and spinning in circles at the sound of Padrino's voice and barking.

"We're good. How are you and Stella?…And hey Tyrin."

"Oh, honey, we're both wore slap out…been a long day, busy as all get out. Just got home an' we're havin' a cold Shiner, 'for we start fixin' supper…Say hydee to Stella."

"Hey, Stella," said Loraine.

"What say, little bit?" asked Bone.

"Hey, Loraine, Bone, ya'll okay?"

"Could say that. Got some info for ya'll…You can close that Lenny Taylor file."

Peach and Stella exchanged looks.

"Who?" asked Stella.

"Lenny Taylor…You know? The guy that killed Joe Jeffers…his boyfriend that had the hots for

Peach, and planted the body next to her while she was asleep?" said Bone.

"And Peach was tried for murder, but my sweet Bone and I figured out it was Lenny? Remember, he knocked the jail guard in the head with his food tray, took his gun and escaped?" added Loraine.

"What?" they both said.

"Bone, bless your heart, but ya'll just ain't makin' a lick of sense," added Peach.

WYNNEWOOD, IT
1899

Bone, Loraine and Padrino exchanged glances before it hit all of them at the same time.

"Uh...Never mind. Explain later...May take a while," said Bone. Give you a call when we get back to the ranch. Laterbye." Bone hit the red phone icon on the screen to kill the call.

"That's heady," said Loraine.

"Lenny never existed anywhere...anytime," commented Padrino.

"Joc Jeffers is still alive, then?" questioned Loraine.

"I'd say," answered Bone, nodding. "Unless he got run over by a bus…Well, what say we take care of Marshal Reeves business here with the bodies and hit the trail. Think I'm ready to get back down to the house, sit down an' have one of those cold beers Fiona keeps down in the well…What do ya'll think?"

"Since you've totally lost me…If ya'll are waitin' on me, you're backin' up…," said Silke.

Loraine laughed. "You've been around Bone too long."

FLYNN RANCH
1899

Bone, Loraine, Padrino, and Silke dismounted at the gate in front of the Flynn's rock house back down in Cooke County, Texas, as Mason, Fiona, Mason's sister Mary Lou and her husband, Cletus Miller, all got to their feet from the rocking chairs they had been sitting in.

Lucy, who had been on the stoop, was already waiting at the gate with Garrin, her blond and white pit bull and Newton, Mason and Fiona's red and white border collie.

"Can't fool you, can we, Lucy?" said Bone as she opened the gate, ran out and jumped up so the big man could pick her up and give her a hug.

"Lucy, this is..." He set her back on the ground.

"Silke Justice, I know Bone...and that's Bear Dog...How do you do, my dear?"

Silke stuck out her hand, but Lucy waved it off and extended both arms to the young woman for a hug.

Silke put Bear Dog down where he promptly jumped up and down, wiggled all over and butted Lucy's leg as she and his mistress embraced.

"An extended hug has many wonderful health benefits, you know," Lucy said after they broke away and she knelt down to love on Bear Dog.

The pup raised up, put both front paws on Lucy's knee and gave her a big kiss across the face.

"I love you, too, Bear Dog," she said as she hugged the pup.

"Let's go up on the porch, Silke...want to introduce you," said Bone.

They stepped up on the porch and he introduced Mason's sister and her husband and then Mason and Fiona.

"…and this is Sheriff Mason Flynn and Deputy US Marshal Fiona Miller Flynn." He nodded at Silke. "Folks, Silke Justice…She's a Pink," said Bone.

"What's a pink, Bone?" asked Mary Lou.

"What we call a female Pinkerton Detective…Fits, don't you think?"

"Oh, my goodness, yes I do…I'm so impressed," responded Mary Lou.

"Thank you, ma'am…" She turned to Fiona and picked up both her hands and held them. "Marshal you've been my idol since I was about fifteen. You're the reason I'm a Pinkerton. Tried to get on with the Marshal's Office, but they said I was too young."

Fiona gave the younger woman a hug. "Thank you, Silke, that's a wonderful compliment."

"She's a darn good law officer, Fiona," added Loraine.

"I'm sure she is, she's got that look in her eyes." Fiona glanced over at Bone and Loraine and grinned. "She doesn't look at you...She looks through you...reads your heart." Fiona nodded.

"Ya'll have a seat, I'll bring out a tray of coffee, a peck bucket of Lone Star, an' some fresh oatmeal an' raisin cookies I just made," said Mary Lou.

"I could smell your cookies when we were riding up, Mary Lou," commented Bone. "Yum."

Bear Dog, Garrin and Newton started playing in the front yard, chasing one another.

"Looks like Bear Dog's fittin' right in," said Silke.

"So, tell me all about the enigma, Bone," commented Lucy.

Bone turned to Silke. "Lucy can read my thoughts from hundreds of miles away."

"Bone is a sender...and, by the way, so are you, Silke...I'm so sorry about your folks," said Lucy.

"Thank you, Lucy, I really appreciate that," said Silke.

"But, Fiona and everyone else is dying to hear about it."

Two plates of cookies, ten bottles of Lone Star beer, and a hour later, Bone, Loraine and Padrino finished telling the sequence of events. Padrino handed Lucy the crystal that was in Lenny's pocket.

"Those who came before us and established the portals, left these for emergency transport."

"So you've seen these before?" asked Bone.

"Oh, yes…It's similiar to our rubies in that it absorbs cosmic energy…I think that's it's also ample evidence that at least ya'll are not on a different timeline or dimension," said Lucy.

"What do you mean?" asked Loraine.

"If you were on a different timeline, then Lenny would still exist in 2019, but since Stella and Peach didn't have any idea what or who you were talking about shows you are on the same plane of existence…and any memory of him is gone for everyone in the future."

"Gives credence to Einstein's theory that the past, present, and the future may well exist at the same time," said Padrino.

"But, if we've always been in the past, how is it that Lenny was ever born?" asked Bone.

Lucy looked at the big man with her wry smile. "That, my dear Bone…will always be the enigma."

§§§§§

REVIEWS

Thank you for reading, *BONE'S ENIGMA*. If you liked it, then you'll want to read the rest of the Bone & Loraine series, beginning with *STEELDUST, BONE, BONE'S LAW, BONE & LORAINE*, and *BONE'S GOLD*. You may also be interested in a spin-off from *BONE'S ENIGMA...SILKE JUSTICE*, due to be released in Oct. of 2019. Just go to my author page: amazon.com/Ken-Farmer/e/B0057OT3YI

But, now, I'd like to ask a favor. Would you please leave a review on Amazon? Just go to the *BONE'S ENIGMA* page, scroll down a little over halfway to the WRITE A CUSTOMER REVIEW button and click on it. The review doesn't need to be long.

Reviews are extremely important to the success of a book. You'll help the ranking of *BONE'S ENIGMA* by leaving a review...Thank you.

AUTHOR'S NOTE

Again, thank you for reading, *BONE'S ENIGMA*, the sixth book in the Bone & Loraine sub-series. I hope you enjoyed it as much as I enjoyed writing it.

I strive for historical accuracy in all of my novels as well as the accurate depiction of horses, horsemanship, tack, firearms, social mores and correct dialogue of the period.

What you will find missing is crude language, explicit sex or any type of overt sexual situations. There always will be a thread of romance in my novels with what I call, behind the door sex, where it belongs. There will be an occasional damn or hell but this was the Victorian era, crude language in front of women was considered rude and was rarely done or tolerated.

I love to hear from my readers. My email is: pagact@yahoo.com and my Facebook page is: www.facebook.com/KenFarmerAuthor/

The first chapter Preview of the spin-off from the *BONE & LORAINE* series, *SILKE JUSTICE* follows on the next page. Silke is a female detective for the Pinkerton Detective Agency…Enjoy.

PREVIEW OF
THE NEXT EXCITING NOVEL
FROM
KEN FARMER

SILKE JUSTICE

CHAPTER ONE

HENRIETTA, TEXAS

"Children, please turn in your readers to page twenty-two…"

Two fifteen year old freckle-faced boys wearing faded blue bib overalls in the back of the room, one on the left side and the other on the right, were throwing a homemade baseball back and forth.

"Boys, stop that," said the prim, attractive strawberry blond teacher at the front of the room.

The two boys ignored her and continued their game of pitch. They had taken a rubber ball and wrapped two inches of kite string tightly around it, making it a serviceable, if a bit rough, ball for their baseball game they played every afternoon.

"I'm not going to say it again, boys…"

The two ruffians continued to ignore the new twenty-three year old substitute teacher.

Some of the other mixed grade students smirked at the two boys doing what they called, 'breakin' in' the new schoolmarm.' None of them noticed the young woman open her desk drawer because they were being entertained watching the pitch and catch across the room at the back.

They all started and several of the girls screamed at the tremendous roar of a handgun discharge from the front of the room, and then as a cloud of white gunsmoke billowed out, the ball flew apart in midair like a shot quail. It fluttered to the floor and bounced twice with the string unraveling until it came to rest.

The entire class jumped to their feet and looked at the hole completely through the homemade ball, sending the string askew.

They turned around and looked at the teacher as she blew the smoke from the muzzle of her ivory-gripped .38-40 Colt Peacemaker and placed it back in her desk drawer. Everyone's eyes were big as saucers and every mouth hung open.

The two boys stood frozen in time for a long moment. They stared at the remains of their ball, looked at each other, and then slowly turned and looked at the teacher with looks of amazement compounded with fear—then awe.

"Now, if I have *everyone's* attention, please turn to page twenty-two of your McGuffey readers," said Elizabeth Longmire—undercover Pinkerton detective, Silke Justice.

As one, and without a word, the class quietly sat down and quickly opened their books.

The one room white clapboard schoolhouse stood at the edge of the Henrietta downtown only a half of a mile from the east to west railroad tracks just south of the Red River.

SILKE JUSTICE

It was a mixed grade school, from seventh through eleventh grades in the morning and one through sixth grades in the afternoon.

A well-dressed man in his thirties boarded the westbound Wichita Falls Railway coal-fired train at the depot in Henrietta. It would join the Missouri-Kansas-Texas Railroad, known as the KATY, in Wichita Falls.

He nodded and tipped his gray Stetson at a middle-aged woman holding the hand of her six-year old daughter as he stood aside and let the pair pass to choose their seats.

"Ma'am."

"Thank you, sir," she responded.

He chose a forward facing seat at the rear of the passenger car and unfolded a copy of the *Clay County Chieftain* newspaper he had picked up in the depot.

The engineer up in the cab of the big black 4x4x2 locomotive released the tall Johnson bar, putting the four-foot tall drive wheels in gear.

They initially slipped a little and then gained purchase on the steel rails and slowly picked up speed as the locomotive chugged out of town, belching a voluminous column of black smoke from its stack.

The train gained speed as it headed west toward Wichita Falls on its short eighteen mile journey across the bucolic countryside of north Texas.

Nine miles out of Henrietta, the train passed through the small community of Jolly and the rear door to the car opened as the blue-clad conductor entered from the caboose.

"Tickets! Have your tickets ready, please."

He turned to the man in the forward-facing seat for his anticipated ticket, but faced the barrel of a .45 caliber Colt Peacemaker.

The passenger got to his feet and stepped behind the frightened conductor and pressed the muzzle against the man's spine.

"Now, stay calm mister…this ain't gonna take too long…I'll have that little shooter you got in yer pocket."

"You won't git away with this, friend," said the conductor as he handed him his .32 caliber, five shot revolver.

"One, I ain't yer friend and two, this ain't my first rodeo."

"Oh! You're the gentleman bandit, ain'tcha?"

He grinned. "That what they're callin' me?"

The conductor nodded.

The robber chuckled and addressed the almost full car. "Folks, this is what's known as a holdup. Don't do anything stupid and this conductor won't get his spine shot in two...You men get out all your cash, wallets, guns an' watches, an' you ladies remove your jewelry. Gonna be passin' along the aisle with a flour sack. Put what you got in it...Wouldn't be smart to hold back, neither."

There were frightened mutterings up and down the car from the mostly business men making their daily commute to the larger city of Wichita Falls.

The bandit moved along the aisleway as the car rocked back and forth, pushing the conductor, with his hands over his head, in front of him. He held out his sack to each side of the aisle for the passengers to drop their valuables in.

One well-dressed man with a gray Homberg hat and carrying a leather valise, held it tightly to his chest.

"Open it," commanded the robber.

"No, no, please," the man protested.

The bandit swung his pistol to the man's forehead and thumbed the hammer back, making ominous clicking sounds.

The business man's head dropped as he opened the valise and took out several wrapped bundles of orange one hundred dollar gold certificate bills stamped, *Payable to Bearer.*

"Just the feller I was lookin' for," said the robber with a grin.

They reached the forward end of the car and suddenly the fiftyish conductor twisted around and attempted to grab the robber's gun. The brigand shoved the muzzle against the man's stomach and pulled the trigger.

Most of the women in the car screamed at the roar of the gunshot as the conductor cried out and collapsed to the floor like so much wet newspaper.

His blue jacket with brass buttons running the length of the garment, burst into flames around the bullet hole, but rapidly went out as blood soaked the cloth. It added the stench of burning wool to the cloud of acrid gunsmoke already filling the closed car.

"This is what stupid gets you." He glanced out the window as the train slowed coming into the outskirts of Wichita Falls.

He tipped his hat to the passengers as he opened the door at the forward end of the car. "Much obliged folks, ya'll have a nice day…Hear?"

The train had slowed to about five miles an hour as it got within a half of a mile from the depot going around a curve in the tracks.

The passengers watched as the outlaw stepped off the steps from the platform to the ground from the slow moving train.

He hurried over to a blood bay gelding being held by another man under a large red oak almost fifty yards from the tracks. The thief handed the sack to the horse holder, stuck his foot in the stirrup and swung into the saddle.

The two road agents spurred their mounts off to the north, with a yell, "Yee-haw."

They galloped out of view of the passengers on the train as it slowed further rounding the curve to the south.

"Good haul?" asked the young man who had been holding his horse as they rode away.

Duce Walton grinned. "You could say so. Boss man's information was right on...The courier was on that train...just like he said."

The children were all exiting the school house for the end of the school day—it was three in the afternoon.

A man in a dark sack cloth suit, wearing a black, uncreased tall crown hat with a red-tail hawk feather stuck into a quill and bead hat band, rode up to the back of the school on a grulla mare—leading a lineback dun. He reined up, stepped down and tied the horses to a hitching rail near the back door. The dust cloud he had generated billowed up behind him, and then began to settle.

Chickasaw Lighthorse, *Nashoba Hommá*, climbed the four steps to the stoop and knocked.

Silke opened the door. "Red Wolf! Let me guess, they hit again."

"Uhh...Wichita train. Got KATY payroll. Knew the man carryin' money was on train."

"Had to be someone on the inside that tipped him off...Same guy?"

"Uhh, him Gentleman Bandit...Kill conductor. Passengers identify from poster...Duce Walton."

Her jaw muscles flexed as Silke ground her teeth. "That's new...Murderin' bastard," she said.

Red Wolf nodded. "Man try grab gun...Not wise."

Silke shook her head as her three month old black wolf-dog pup, Bear Dog came out from under her desk when she and Red Wolf came inside. "I'm goin' to catch him, God as my witness...He's mine. Been on his tail since the Tackett gang killed momma and daddy...He's the only one that hasn't paid the piper."

She had already changed from her schoolmarm outfit to her trail clothing—blue denim pants with a tan leather seat insert, dark burgundy three-button shirt and blue denim jacket. She had ordered a set of doeskins like Bone and Loraine wore, but hadn't gotten them yet. They were being custom made for her by Deputy US Marshal Fiona Flynn's grandmother in Tahlequah, Cherokee Nation.

Silke was in expectation of *Nashoba Hommá's* arrival and had released her long reddish-blond tresses from the constraining bun at the back of her head to a thick, loose, single braid that draped over her left shoulder.

Silke Justice had been hired by the Missouri-Kansas-Texas Railroad through the Pinkerton Detective Agency to track down Walton for a rash of train robberies across north Texas and the southern Indian Nations.

She had gotten her friend and mentor, Red Wolf, on loan from the Chickasaw Lighthorse Police force because Duce's trail often led back across the Red and into the Chickasaw Nation.

"You leave school, now?" asked Red Wolf.

She nodded. "The regular teacher is due back tomorrow from visiting her momma in Dennison, who was ill, so I'm good to go…Where did the tracks lead?"

"Get off train outside Wichita Falls. Someone there with horse as usual…Head north, cross Red into Oklahoma Territory at Thornberry."

Silke nodded. "What I was afraid of…Knew KATY was tryin' to sneak the money to Wichita Falls with an undercover courier instead of an armed shipment in the express car…'cause that hadn't worked very well in the past…Somebody in the know told that scum."

She hesitated a moment, and then continued, "Need to find out where they're makin' the hand off…and to who…We get Duce Walton, they'll just get somebody else to do their dirty work. Need to cut the head off the snake."

§§§

OTHER NOVELS FROM
TIMBER CREEK PRESS
www.timbercreekpress.net

MILITARY ACTION/TECHNO

BLACK EAGLE FORCE: Eye of the Storm (Book #1)
by Buck Stienke and Ken Farmer

BLACK EAGLE FORCE: Sacred Mountain (Book #2) by Buck Stienke and Ken Farmer

RETURN of the STARFIGHTER (Book #3)
by Buck Stienke and Ken Farmer

BLACK EAGLE FORCE: BLOOD IVORY (Book #4)
by Buck Stienke and Ken Farmer with Doran Ingrham

BLACK EAGLE FORCE: FOURTH REICH (Book #5) by Buck Stienke and Ken Farmer

AURORA: INVASION (Book #6 in the BEF) by Ken Farmer & Buck Stienke

BLACK EAGLE FORCE: ISIS (Book #7) by Buck Stienke and Ken Farmer

BLOOD BROTHERS - Doran Ingrham, Buck Stienke and Ken Farmer

DARK SECRET - Doran Ingrham

NICARAGUAN HELL - Doran Ingrham

BLACKSTAR BOMBER by T.C. Miller

BLACKSTAR BAY by T.C. Miller
BLACKSTAR MOUNTAIN by T.C. Miller
BLACKSTAR ENIGMA by T.C. Miller

HISTORICAL FICTION WESTERN
THE NATIONS by Ken Farmer and Buck Stienke
HAUNTED FALLS by Ken Farmer and Buck Stienke
HELL HOLE by Ken Farmer
ACROSS the RED by Ken Farmer and Buck Stienke
BASS and the LADY by Ken Farmer and Buck Stienke
DEVIL'S CANYON by Buck Stienke
LADY LAW by Ken Farmer
BLUE WATER WOMAN by Ken Farmer
FLYNN by Ken Farmer
AURALI RED by Ken Farmer
COLDIRON by Ken Farmer
STEELDUST by Ken Farmer
BONE by Ken Farmer
BONE'S LAW by Ken Farmer
BONE & LORAINE by Ken Farmer
BONE'S GOLD by Ken Farmer
BONE'S PARADOX by Buck Stienke
BONE'S ENIGMA by Ken Farmer

SY/FY
LEGEND of AURORA by Ken Farmer & Buck
Stienke
AURORA: INVASION (Book #6 in the BEF) by
Ken Farmer & Buck Stienke

HISTORICAL FICTION ROMANCE
THE TEMPLAR TRILOGY
MYSTERIOUS TEMPLAR by Adriana Girolami
THE CRIMSON AMULET by Adriana Girolami
TEMPLAR'S REDEMPTION by Adriana Girolami

Coming Soon

HISTORICAL FICTION WESTERN
NO TIME to DIE by Buck Stienke (sequel to
Devil's Canyon by Buck Stienke
SILKE JUSTICE by Ken Farmer

HISTORICAL FICTION ROMANCE
DAUGHTER of HADES by Adriana Girolami
ZAMINDAR and the LADY by Adriana Girolami

SY/FY
ANTAREAN DILEMMA by T.C. Miller

Thanks for reading *BONE'S ENIGMA* If you enjoyed it, I would really appreciate a review on Amazon. My Author Page is:

www.amazon.com/Ken-Farmer/e/B0057OT3YI

Email - pagact@yahoo.com

Personally autographed books available at my web site:

Web page: www.KenFarmer-Author.net

TIMBER CREEK PRESS

Made in the USA
Middletown, DE
14 June 2019